The Young and the Brave

Rifleman Parton was an inexperienced replacement; Private Ryder was the battle-weary soldier forced to take him under his wing.

"Why don't they send us a *soldier*?" Ryder asked the others sarcastically. "It isn't asking too goddam much to want a soldier out here, is it?"

"Take it easy, Ryder, for Christ's sake. He's just a kid," one of them said.

"I don't give a damn," Ryder responded. "Is the goddam army so crazy it thinks *this* can ever replace the likes of . . .?"

Stung beyond endurance, nineteen-year-old Parton had to prove himself to the others. "Any time you want to find out how good I am," he told Ryder, "we can square off and I'll show you."

We will send you a free catalog on request. Any titles not in your local book store can be purchased by mail. Send the price of the book, plus 50¢ shipping charge to Belmont Tower Books, Two Park Avenue, New York, New York 10016.

Titles currently in print are available in quantity for industrial and sale promotion use at reduced rates. Address inquiries to our Promotion Department.

HEROES DIE YOUNG

Rick Sandford

BELMONT TOWER BOOKS • NEW YORK CITY

A BELMONT TOWER BOOK

Published by

Tower Publications, Inc.
Two Park Avenue
New York, N.Y. 10016

Copyright © 1979 by Tower Publications, Inc.

All rights reserved
Printed in the United States of America

1

In that particular war, one miracle would repeat itself over and over again. A citizen would be taken out of his everyday life and sent to the Army—and there he would become a man.

Now a man isn't some hairy-chested guy who can curse in seven languages and make a muscle the size of an M-1 rifle. And a man isn't somebody who carries pictures of Betty Grable with him and can tell stories that make someone of the same sex whistle with envy. Those people are only males—that is to say, humans built in such a way that they get called by a title which ought to be used only in referring to a *special* kind of person.

You don't have to be born male to be a man, either. For instance, there was a woman during the early part of the war, in '43, who plucked her husband from prison camp before the Nazis could kill him. To this day it isn't known how she pulled it off, but she was more man than dozens of circus strong-men or prizefighters or so-called athletes or even a few generals of the army, if the truth be told.

A man is somebody who knows that he might just possibly die in a short time and accepts it and goes about the work of living in the best way he's able. He doesn't have to live by the Boy Scout oath, but he doesn't take advantage of other people, either, using them to sharpen his ego. It helps if he's brave, but its more important to know the meaning of fear, to feel it, to live with it. In that way, he won't take chances unless he has to. Running in front of a bull with shaved horns is only playing at bravery. Fighting a weakened bull in a ring is playing at it, too, even if you have the bad luck to be injured. What he needs most of all is the desire to make things better even though he knows very well just what is happening and what might happen. A man is somebody who doesn't tell himself lies.

That sharpened sense of it-has-to-be-done seems to have been developed in a lot of men from the Sixteenth Army Corps. Whether it's the bookkeeper who fought at San Juan Hill, the druggist who shucked an arm at Ypres, or so many others, they all lived with the conviction of duty that had to be done. They believed in a dozen different true gods and in the needs of the moment. They wanted to go home, but fought because it had to be done. And they fought well. They fought like demons and ducked away from death as long and hard as they could. Many died in any number of nasty ways, but without feeling guilty on account of things they hadn't done. Each one had acquired the right to die without guilt feelings because each had been a man.

Of course the Sixteenth was in the E.T.O. during World War Two, fighting, dying, losing weapons and arms and legs and eyes—and above all engaging in the time-honored business of manufacturing men.

Take, for instance, Jeff Parton.

2

Jeff eased the rifle strap onto a thin shoulder and jumped out of the truck. As soon as his feet hit the dark brown mud, he could smell its warmth along with sweet wine and fresh human waste. A big gun firing in the distance made a noise that still reminded Jeff of cracking tin.

A tent stood some fifty feet away. Jeff straightened up to his best parade-ground posture before coming close to it, even though he didn't see a guard. He had decided months ago that he for one wasn't going to be taken off-balance by anything that members of the U.S. Army might pull to keep a new arrival on his toes. The warm ooze of mud climbed into his boots with every precise step, making him grit his teeth.

When Jeff got inside the tent, he found a heavyset platoon sergeant scowling down at papers on a rickety wooden table. The table had been nicked at the left corner, and seven or eight match burns had been made in the wood to form the letters SHI and the crossbar of a T. Jeff stopped himself from asking why a sergeant at the command post of Baker Company of the Third Battalian of the Sixteenth Army Corps had to work at such a beat-up old table. He had been in uniform long enough to know that a soldier didn't ask questions about what was damned well none of his business.

He tried to wipe dirt off one slim hand in the same way that a dog might flick moisture from its body. With that done, he opened his breast pocket and pulled out the folded transfer papers.

"Parton, huh?" The sergeant skimmed through the printed-and-typed forms and looked Jeff up and down with eyes the same color as that mud now on the inside of his boots. "You British?"

"My parents came from there, Sir."

"I'm not supposed to be called *Sir*."

"Sorry."

"They should'a told you during the two minutes basic training you got that I'm not supposed to be called *Sir*. Okay, kid, now answer my question right."

"My people came from England."

"How old are you?"

"Nineteen."

"Are you really nineteen, or fifteen with a long tongue?"

"I'm really nineteen."

"Christ in a basket, but I hope so, even if it only gives me less paperwork to do. Last week I had to send some hell-raising G.I. home to the States because it turned out he was only fifteen years old. He'd raised hell with Fritz already, and he sure hated to go."

"Damn fool!"

"What did you say, kid?"

"I'm sorry. I couldn't help myself."

"Okay, kid, your control slipped for once. But what did you say?"

"That the fifteen-year-old you were talking about is a damn fool."

"Yeh, kid, you look like you'd probably run as soon as you got the chance, but I hope you wouldn't screw up your buddies."

"I'd try not to give anybody a hard time, Sergeant, but I wouldn't volunteer for anything, either."

"Well, you might make a soldier at that," the Sergeant decided surprisingly. "Anybody who wouldn't volunteer has got the right stuff in him. Of course you'd need plenty of help before you could get the inside track on soldiering, like recognizing your left foot from your right on a clear day."

Jeff said rigidly, "I went through basic at Fort Bragg, Sergeant, and—"

"I saw what it says in your record, kid. Three cheers and a month's supply of fish heads for you. Now where do you hail from originally?"

"New York City."

"Kid, why do you keep telling me shit that I can read on these here sheets?"

"I'm sorry—Sergeant."

"You've got the makings of a real three-footed soldier, kid, unless somebody takes you in hand. When I asked where you hail from I meant where did you live before Uncle got hold of you."

"In the borough of Queens, at—"

"Okay, that's enough. I used to know a piece of tail in Brooklyn is what makes me ask."

"I see."

"Now that I've explained everything until it's coming out of my ears you finally see. You're liable to catch on to something just ten seconds too late and send your platoon into the hole. I'm not saying you're stupid, kid. Not a damn bit. Just that while you're on your guard and scared pissless somebody's gonna roust you. That's the wrong way to be when you aren't in action."

"I suppose so."

"But I guess you'll be all right, kid, under one condition. You sure as hell are gonna need a rabbi."

"But Sergeant, I'm not Jewish. If the records say I am, they've got to be changed."

"Relax and don't give me a hard time, kid, or you won't be let to see Bob Hope."

"But Serg—"

"And he's not alone, either. Frances Langford is with him. You've been told about pretty girls, haven't you?"

Jeff tried to clear his throat as the tent flap was wrenched open by another sergeant. This one was almost as tall and thin as Jeff himself and couldn't have been five years older.

The newcomer asked, "Everything copasettic?"

"Okay so far," the heavyset one said agreeably. "You can take over with my compliments after I finish work with this one from the new batch, the replacements."

Jeff shifted the weight of his M-1 on a shoulder. "There's a mistake in my records!"

"Oh, I forgot about that." The heavyset Sergeant grinned at his co-worker. "Rifleman Parton over here claims he won't need a rabbi because he ain't Yiddish."

"Hitler will be disappointed."

"Kid, hear me good. You're gonna need a rabbi as much as anybody I ever heard tell about, and if you're lucky you'll get a tough and mean rabbi. Now shut up and put your helmet on straight, kid. And move your ass. I'm taking you to the war!"

The army had caught Jeff off-balance after all, as he had fearfully expected. The heavyset sergeant was whistling under his breath ("Don't sit under the apple tree" was the tune, and he didn't sing any worse than the Andrews Sisters) as he led the way along a rocky footpath under tall trees while Jeff wished fervently that the mistake hadn't happened.

Enemy gunfire was closer than he'd ever heard it as the sergeant led him up a short hill—even the earth in France smelled like it had been dipped in wine—and stopped so suddenly that Jeff would have bumped into him if he hadn't been taking every step with great care.

"Look for Sergeant O'Caffie and don't tell him your folks were British," the heavyset one said. "He'll show you the ropes. Good luck, kid."

By the time a shamefaced Jeff was trying to thank the Sergeant, that heavyset man was on his way back to the tent.

A Boeing overhead briefly blotted out the sun's rays. When light was restored, Jeff saw a G.I. with helmet in hand wiping his forehead with a dirty handkerchief.

"I'm looking for Sergeant O'Caffie."

"He's around someplace. I'm Arthur Finger."

"Can you tell me where the sergeant is? There's some kind of mistake in my record, and I have to get it cleared up before I do anything else."

"What would that be, fella?"

"The sergeant who brought me over kept saying that I'll need a rabbi, and I'm not Jewish."

Arthur Finger wiped his mouth with the back of a hand. "I'll send O'Caffie over if I find him, kid." Finger walked off, tired, feet outspread, helmet tilted far down. The helmet dropped. Finger bent down slowly, raised the helmet, and had to take another half a dozen steps before he could straighten up. His back was a little stiffer than before, as if raising up that helmet had been a triumph for a man so tired.

For a while Jeff felt as if he didn't belong anywhere in this world. He had found his way to nowhere, with nothing, and would spend the rest of his life making believe he was part of an active community of well-adjusted people. Sure he was! And he was Fred Astaire, too, just waiting for Ginger Rogers!

The shivers would have taken complete control if he hadn't felt himself being looked at. He turned his head warily. A couple of men were sitting in a clearing, where the grass must have been chopped down to accommodate them. There was a sandbag nearby, and one of the men leaned against it, looking like somebody fast asleep at third base on Ebbets Field in the middle of a game.

Seeing Jud's eyes on him, the soldier asked, "When did you leave the States?"

"Three weeks ago."

"Yeh? Then you wouldn't know."

"Know about what?"

"If it's true that Roosevelt died in a plane crash."

"I would think it'd be broadcast on radio if it was true."

"All you ever get out here is Axis Sally, but the music is good."

The subject had been exhausted.

Jeff asked, "Do you know where I can find Sergeant O'Caffie? It's important."

The soldier who had talked to him shrugged off the question. The other one couldn't have cared less.

Jeff walked to the end of the clearing, where man-high grass sentinels stood. He touched a blade of the stuff, and it wouldn't bend. Pressure turned the skin of his left forefinger muddy gray, then a sickly yellow. His gun was on the ready, and he tried to concentrate on finding Sergeant O'Caffie. Back of him the men talked with voices like files across steel.

On a patch of earth some ten feet from the other side of a man-high bush, a human shadow was moving toward him.

Automatically he did what he had been taught, reaching over to his right shoulder for the M-1. He felt that his brains were shaking, not his hands, at the prospect of his first kill. He supposed he'd had the notion that once he learned how to kill he'd never have to do it.

The other man seemed to have pulled out a shiny black handgun just before Jeff came face to face with him. An American in uniform, Jeff saw with silent gratitude, a tall and hatchetfaced man whose eyes pierced Jeff with quick contempt,

"Adolf looks different from me, you little jerk," the American said, easing the handgun into a side pocket. "Don't play any goddam games, junior, and quit crappin' in your pants."

Without waiting for Jeff to put the rifle back in place, the man turned sharply to one side and walked through a gap he had made between the grass shoots. The voices of the other soldiers soared amiably.

"Hey, Ryder, where the hell you been?" the rasping one demanded. "Turning your back to Jerry and daring him to do something about it?"

"I ain't lost my marbles yet."

"With you, Ryder, nobody can tell. You're just plumb crazy all the time."

"If you shmucks really want to know, I hitched a ride to Carcassonne and got—this!"

He brandished a bottle with a green label and a watery red liquid inside.

"Looks like Indian piss."

"The hell with that! Anybody who can get the Frenchies to give away or even sell a bottle in '44 is a goddam genius."

"You're not kidding," the man named Ryder said.

"Hey, now I think about brains, who's that crazy kid over there? So goddam efficient he's probably on Ike's staff, or an exec. He's got to be an exec, a showboat like him."

"Forget him," the raspy-voiced one said.

Jeff, irritated, put in pointedly, "I'm new around here, a replacement, and I want to know where I can find . . ."

Ryder's hatchet-face grew dark in a sneer. "Replacement?" All his former rugged amiability was gone. "Is the fuckin' army so crazy it thinks *this* can ever make up for the likes of . . .?"

"Ryder, they've got to send us something."

"Why don't they send a soldier to replace Burris Barnes? It isn't asking too goddam much to want a soldier out here, is it?"

Jeff, standing less than six feet from the tall summer grass in this wide field under a late afternoon sky that was changing to the color of an inflamed sore, felt as if he had too many fingers on each hand. A spiky blade of grass raked the tip of his left ear, but instead of caring for the trivial cut he stood in one place as if he'd been frozen.

"Burris Barnes was the best we ever had!" Ryder snapped. "Just because he buys himself some real estate out here, the Army don't have to send this—this crap over, instead!"

"Take it easy, Ryder, for Christ's sweet sake! He's a kid, and he don't know a hell of a lot. I'm sorry old Burris bought it, too, but we can't do nothing about it."

The other one added quietly, "There's been a whole new flock of replacements coming out, and we got at least one. That's all there is to it."

Anger had taken the place of embarrassment now. For the first time Jeff let himself take the measure of this sworn enemy. Six-feet-two and big as a factory foreman that Jeff used to know, Ryder's arms bulged under dirt-pocked khaki. His reach was almost certainly longer that Jeff's. At twenty-five, for a guess, there didn't seem to be an extra ounce of weight on him. Close-in combat with this man was sure to be bruising, and to ask for it might be the quickest known way of committing suicide.

Stung almost beyond endurance, and with the nineteen-year-old's powerful desire to prove himself in front of other people, Jeff took the offensive.

"Any time you want to find out how good I am, we can square off and I'll show you."

One of the soldiers held out a hand in front of Ryder, as if to keep him in place. "You'd walk all over him, Gil. It'd be a massa-cree."

"Name the place and the time," Jeff insisted, his voice becoming louder as the big experienced rifleman stayed quiet. "You can bring your own cheering section if you won't feel right without 'em."

Ryder finally pressed a palm up to his mouth, and it didn't occur to Jeff till much later that the big man was covering a grimly amused smile.

"Okay, junior, you made your point."

Jeff tried to keep his jaw from dropping in surprise.

"You took a calucated risk and figured that a guy as big as me wouldn't waste his advantages in height and speed and strength on a puny looking kid, so you could show the three of us that you're as brave as hell and wouldn't have to worry about a fight. You're cagey, but a kid isn't able to do a man's work here or anyplace else."

Jeff said reasonably, "We're stuck with each other—so why don't we make the best of it?"

"You're stuck with me and the rest of us. I'm not stuck with a snot-ass kid."

Ryder's voice grew thoughtful just as Jeff turned away. "I'll make a deal, though."

Jeff said sullenly, "Don't do me no favors."

"I'm not. You'll have to do something, too, but it'll keep both of us healthier. On my part, kid, I'll get off your back. In fact, I won't cut into you at all until your war is over one way or the other."

"What's my part of the deal?" Jeff asked, noticing that Ryder didn't doubt he himself would make it to war's end.

"I expect you not to talk to me at all. I don't even want to see Burris Barnes' replacement, kid, if I can help it. Is that perfectly clear?"

The raspy-voiced soldier said awkwardly and unnecessarily, "The guy you're replacing was a pal of Ryder's."

"We've got a deal," Jeff said to Ryder, bitterly aware that the man might be called on to save his life some day. "We can agree to it by not shaking hands."

Ryder, angered by such childlike bravado, shouted, "Shut your fuckin' little mouth, starting now!"

Another man heard Ryder's thundering voice. The newcomer called out with authority, "Keep it down, you men—and wait there for me!"

Jeff's attention was distracted only slightly by the tinny burst of an eighty-eight millimeter shell in the distance. The sound annoyed him without shocking him—he supposed he'd already heard the sound without noticing it. Was he going to get used to it along with the sounds of death and the casual brutality of war?

The newcomer, hurrying in a gingerly way across ten feet of cleared ground to where the four of them stood, was a medium-sized and thick-bodied man with a broad nose and heavy lips. The right sleeve of his jacket was decorated with a sergeant's stripes.

"Have you seen the new m—?" the three-striper started, then smiled at Jeff. There was a split second between his first sight of Jeff and the smile, but the sergeant nearly managed to look as if Jeff was exactly the kind of new man he had been hoping to see. "I'm Sergeant O'Caffie."

"Private Parton, Jeffrey Parton."

The Sergeant didn't make any remark about a British-sounding name. "Is the prima donna giving you a hard time? Ryder, I mean."

"No, we were just talking."

He glanced out of the corner of an eye, knowing that it was too damn calculating on his part, to see how the other soldiers responded to his generosity in keeping the grievance to himself. They seemed to be silently approving.

"Good thing there's no trouble." The sergeant's roaming eyes stopped pointedly at sight of the long-necked bottle on the ground close to one of the newspapers. "You men had better get that shit out of sight by sacktime."

Ryder asked casually, "Are we taking a trip tomorrow?"

"Patrol, but I can't guarantee you'll run into the jerries."

Jeff wanted to ask what the sergeant really meant. In the Army, men were always making the little everyday irritations sound as if the world would come to an end on account of them. He drew a deep breath.

O'Caffie's attention was caught. "You won't be left alone, son." He glanced at the other. "This kid won't have a chance in hell if somebody with experience doesn't take him under a wing and keep an eye on him.

You men probably remember what it was like to be green, except for Ryder who was born with a rifle over his shoulder. The point is that the kid needs a rabbi and needs it pretty bad."

At any other time Jeff would've laughed. So that particular word referred only to an advisor, somebody who'd show the ropes to a replacement with no direct combat experience. He supposed he'd tell his folks about it when he wrote home.

Better yet it made him feel a little more chipper to know that these men would help him take care of himself as much as possible.

But the sergeant's next few words wiped out gratitude and satisfaction, let alone amusement. His eyes rested on one particular soldier, now.

"This kid needs the biggest, the toughest, and the strongest guy, somebody who's able to watch out for a kid and take care of himself, too."

Ryder asked quietly, "What's all this, sergeant? Here it is—only August, and already I can feel snow all over."

"I want you to be the kid's rabbi, Ryder. I want you to stick close and take care of him as much as you can."

"Now hold on just a fuckin' minute, there!"

"That's an order, Ryder. Play around with it and God help you because the Army sure as hell won't."

3

The sergeant walked back toward the Command Post so quickly he couldn't have heard any complaints.

One of the other men put a hand on Ryder's shoulder and spoke calmly while Jeff obeyed a signal from the other and kept his lips buttoned.

The raspy-voiced man led him away, taking Jeff in charge and introducing him to a war front for the first time. Nothing could have been more like what he had been shown and told about back in training, but it took him by surprise all the same. Now it was real.

From the top of a rise he could see a lot of it. Back of him were trees that looked like giant toothpicks with leaves. When he looked slightly upward he could see the watchtowers and men with machine guns, men always on the alert for any sign of the Germans. Jeff hadn't been in the Army long enough to get over a feeling of raw fear when he was close to men who carried loaded weapons, no matter whose side they might be on. The back of his neck prickled.

In front of him was a barrier made up of loose coils of barbed wire fastened at intervals to steel stakes. A number of mines had been planted between rows of the wire, catching glints of hard sun and cruelly reflecting it.

At night, his two guides led him to gun pits lined with sandbags. He and the others would be here till dawn. Jeff eased the M-1 off his right shoulder, thanked the two men who had helped him, and stood looking out at the pitch-dark night, ears cocked to catch any sound different from the whir of crickets. Ryder's laugh was inspired by his overeagerness, but Jeff didn't move.

Jeff was surprised to hear himself stifling a yawn. Well, things had been rough for him these last few days. He'd gotten to France along with other men he had known at basic. Everybody said that it was possible to spend as much as a whole month waiting around for some assignment. What with red tape and all, the war operations were pretty screwed up. Jeff had met one man who'd been back in the same place for five months and showed no desire to land an assignment. It bothered the others that different riflemen were going out on every side. And then there had been another man shifted here after D-Day, and going through his third month of what he referred to as dynamic passivity.

"I spend all my free time in the town of Huitieme, if you know it," he had told Jeff. "I'm helpin' the natives improve their lot economically by puttin' up a new whorehouse for the town."

"Is that all you can think to do?"

"Shee-yit, no! I'm helpin' with their spiritual side, too, or I will as soon a bunch of us start rebuilding the church.

"And that's your priority list? The whorehouse first and then the church—is that what you're telling me?"

"Me and the mayor, both. He's pestering the Army for the top-priority item in his list, and not getting anywhere."

"What is it he wants?"

"Mirrors for the whorehouse."

Jeff had pulled a replacement assignment only

three days after getting to France and getting his fill of war news. All he had heard, in hundreds of different variations, was that Ike was turning back from the Breton ports and circling the German Seventh Army and Panzer group, an outfit headed by German Field Marshall Von Kluge. Jeff's father probably knew more about how the war was going than he did.

It had now been a whole day since he had seen anybody he knew well. No wonder he was on edge being alone with so damn many strangers.

None of this would be going into his letters. He would tell the folks instead that everything was fine. When he had been on leave after basic, his father had complained to him about writing letters that didn't say anything. His mother kept asking about the little things, figuring that if the food was all right and there were drapes on the barracks windows, then army life couldn't be all bad.

And then there was Marilyn. He supposed that he wouldn't have let himself get so close to her if it hadn't been for the fear that he might not come back, so that he needed to know that there was some girl in Queens who missed him. He didn't love Marilyn. Hell, he probably wouldn't have recognized love if it had been served to him on the chow line.

One of the soldiers said, "We can all use a little sack time."

Jeff stretched out on his blanket across a corner of the hole, and to his later surprise managed to get some sleep. When he was awakened again in two hours he felt as if he had been roasted alive.

A soldier said to him, "You should have shmeered bug juice on you, kid. It keeps those crappers away."

"Next time I will," Jeff said fervently.

Twenty minutes past dawn he heard the growling-dog sound that always came before the appearance of the chow truck. The sounds of food being crunched between stiff jaws could be heard for quite a few minutes afterwards, along with the slurp-slurp of drinking and the opening and closing of canteens. Each man carried two of those.

"Let's the hell get busy," Sergeant O'Caffie said, his voice at least as strong as the noise he was talking against. "Break up the cocktail party and let's haul ass."

Jeff reached for his M-1, pulled the bolt back, opened the cover, made sure that there was ammo in the feeder, then closed the cover and snapped the safety. Those precautions cost him a chance to talk with O'Caffie, but the Sergeant paid no attention. His big nose looked red at the tip, and the tips of his ears looked red as well. The Sergeant had probably been chewed out by some of the brass.

Jeff and the others went to help fight a war. In front of the platoon CP was a jeep, and two men in it rode behind the moving men. The hatchet-faced soldier moved suddenly to Jeff's right, between Jeff and Ryder, who had been on the point of moving before he noticed who was there. O'Caffie narrowed his eyes thoughtfully, glancing from Ryder to Jeff.

"Ex-lax, kid," a GI told Jeff. "How goes it?"

"Okay, I think."

"You haven't got the shits, have you?"

"No."

"Scared."

"I suppose so."

"Well, there's no reason why you shouldn't be. Them krauts are mean bastards and with lots of equinment, too. Where'd you do basic, kid?"

"Bragg."

"I was at Bliss myself, but if you're doing basic all of them places are pretty much the same. You're in the army, and it's like being part of a watch and you can get put anyplace and there's no difference."

"I guess so."

"Bet your ass it's so. Look what happened to me once in basic up at Bliss. We were marching in formation, straight ahead, the pack of us. And there was a big pool of water right in front. Well, the guys with me in line marched so as not to get their GI's wet. Me, well I wasn't exactly wearing a zoot soot with a reet pleat, but I figured I was gonna be different. For once in my life I wouldn't be part of the machine. So I walked right into the water."

"I'll bet you caught holy hell."

"I wish I had," Jeff's new friend said quietly and bitterly. "It turned out that the CO had wanted everybody should walk into the water and obey orders blindly, meaning that I'd been the joe who behaved like part of the machine."

"Sorry about that."

He and his friend were the only two who weren't chewing. Cookie crumbs, sugar cubes, even French bread was being chewed. Ryder had passed up a chance to take food and was drinking from his canteen instead. The hard-faced soldier was walking a respectful distance from the other.

The purring sounds he made were enough to alert O'Caffie. The Sergeant sniffed at the canteen, and emptied good wine to the earth. Then he said roughly, "You must think you're Superman, Ryder, if you figure you can tank up with wine and mess with krauts and look out for a green kid."

"I could clean up a town, and do it single-o."

"Don't bet on it, shithead." O'Caffie had seen the

look on Jeff's face, and now he spoke a little more loudly. "I suppose you want another rabbi."

Jeff shrugged.

"Kid, I'm assigning you to Mort over there. Do what he tells you and you'll be okay. Mort isn't an apprentice wino like the lone wolf over here."

Mort was the friendly soldier near him, a fellow who would have been flat-faced except for what was known in Queens as a Jewish nose. Experienced as Mort whatever-his-name might have been, Jeff couldn't keep anxiety from gnawing at him.

"Did you hear," somebody asked, "that jerry is supposed to have a secret weapon?"

"Yeh, they're gonna play records of Adolf's speeches and it'll put everybody to sleep."

"No, shit, if those bastards have really got anything—"

"If they do, you'll find out if you live that long."

Mort smiled again at Jeff. "Don't worry, kid. In no time at all, your cherry will be busted."

"Single file," O'Caffie said, lowering his voice. "And haul ass."

The slight change gave Jeff time to see that there was a radio man with them, and a photographer and another stranger who he supposed was a reporter. A soapy grit seemed to be attacking his eyes as he walked with the others. He saw short grass and tall trees, money-colored and somehow smelling of wine, which was impossible. A marsh had to be navigated, and Jeff didn't think he had ever seen so many tree stumps. His eyes moved from left to right in endless search for men he had never known and who wanted to kill him.

O'Caffie pointed sharply ahead. "There!"

The ground sloped away at about a twenty-degree angle, and a well-worn dirt path led past grass and knee-high bushes to a double line of frame houses.

"That's the village of Lumaire," O'Caffie said, purposely mispronouncing it, as if to keep his distance in some small way from this war. Jeff noticed that the jeep carrying officers wasn't in sight any longer. "We know Fritz has been here and he might still be. Now go in there and dig out the bastards once and for all."

And he added, "Kid, I want you between Mort and Ryder, with Mort in front. Hurry!"

The moves were made swiftly and silently. Jeff wondered if it was Ryder he heard wheezing in back of him. He kept a hand tightly along the bone of his narrow jaw, to prevent himself from looking around at the man and measuring him for the second time in two days. He could hear his own hard breathing.

"All set," O'Caffie said. "Good luck."

Jeff had to force himself to keep five yards from Mort as he walked into this strange and possibly hostile town. Making him keep his distance from others seemed like the worst indignity that the army had forced on him to date. His fears made him furious at the army, at Ryder, and at himself. Wherever he looked he saw grass, trees, dust, and dirt.

As the squad walked into the village he could feel eyes staring at him even though he didn't see a living human being except for other soldiers. He knew that the people of this village dreaded the worst.

Mort said, "Come with me, kid."

He flushed some people out of homes. Keeping Jeff behind him, he escorted them to a control point already designated by O'Caffie—in this case a building at the farthest corner. Behind the building was a well of cool water. For a moment Mort told him to wait. Jeff glanced around to make sure there wasn't any trouble, then advanced to the water well and picked up a much-used tin cup. He stood hesitating when he heard a wail behind him. He turned to see an old woman coming closer. She drew the cup gently out of his hand, jabbering in the local lingo.

A young woman nursing a baby suddenly withdrew the baby's mouth from one of the wet red nipples and gave the water to her baby.

Mort called out, "Here, kid!"

Jeff did as he was told, running along the double line of homes. Mort had taken a position just to the right of the open door, then fired half a dozen shots inside. He ran into it as Jeff watched and heard him call out some words in a guttural tongue that he took to be German.

Jeff followed gingerly, wondering if he hadn't already waited too long. He walked into what had once been a home. The walls were bare, and except for a bed and a shaky table there wasn't a single thing in it that reminded him even slightly of anything he would associate with a living place. One of Mort's bullets had made the table sway, and Jeff was in time to see it fall against Mort and knock him off his pins. Mort was turning and struggling to get up, shifting the heavy table, when Jeff reached him.

"My right leg hurts like hell," Mort said when Jeff had raised the table and hurled it against a wall.

Despite the fear in him, Jeff couldn't help thinking that no such incident was likely to happen to a man like Ryder. "I'll get help."

"Don't take any chances, kid."

Jeff opened the door onto the mechanical stutter of gunfire and a voice saying with fierce pride, "Either I got the bastard or there's a load of wine bottles with bullet wounds."

A soldier was walking with cat strides toward the nearest home, and as Jeff peered around he heard a door kicked open and shots fired inside. A man peered in, walked inside, said a few sharp words in guttural German, and walked out. The harsh voice belonged to Ryder.

He couldn't think of any alternative to asking Gil Ryder for help. Ryder, standing past the battered doorway of the next house, glanced at Jeff with familiar tired contempt in those hard features.

"You and Burris Barnes." There was no inflection in his face. "Barney is probably doing handstands right now if he knows what a good replacement he's got."

"I'll handle my share of the job as soon as they let me," Jeff responded quickly and angrily. "I came to tell you that Mort needs med help. A table fell in on him."

"Slob." Ryder was thinking quickly. "Can Mort take care of any jerry who shows up?"

"I think so."

"Okay, then. He'll keep."

"You mean you aren't going to help get the medic to him?" Jeff was almost open-mouthed. "He's having a rough time in there."

"Shut up," Ryder said thinly. "I'm stuck with you for a while whether I like it or not so you come with me. But keep your hole shut, no matter what else you do."

He turned for the next house. A chunk of wood had fallen across his path. Jeff started to warn the man against stubbing a toe and felt surprised that he should think of helping Ryder avoid even a minor injury. Ryder booted the wood out of his path before Jeff managed to say a word.

The sun had shifted slightly as he stepped outside back of Ryder. The more experienced soldier signalled

Jeff to keep his distance. Jeff's eyes roamed the village, but he didn't see Sergeant O'Caffie or anybody else at the moment. He wished his nostrils weren't so aware of the smells of wine, bitter cheese, mud, dirt, wet wood and dry cloth.

Ryder paused. Over a shoulder he said:

"Stay there, deadhead!"

It was too much for Jeff. He ran into the house past an open-mouthed Ryder, firing as he ran. Ryder's sudden profanity clawed at Jeff's eardrums, and so did the sound of his own raised voice calling in English for every German to surrender. The home had been blasted so much that it looked like a bowling alley with every pin knocked sideways.

Ryder, fists on hip and forehead creased by a scowl, was standing alertly just inside the door.

"Don't do that again!" he snapped. "I'm not going to take the risk of some more men getting reamed just because a snotnose kid wants to prove he's a hero."

Jeff felt his face grow warm with anger. Ryder's glare amounted to unspoken profanity. Even the man's receding chin looked as if it could turn into a weapon.

"And I don't want you shooting that fucker off, either." He tapped the M-1 with a forefinger. "You tried to puncture me yesterday, and I'm not letting you hit any one of our guys for real. I can handle Fritz, and if you so much as fire one shot while you're with me I'll let you have a bullet in the back—FOC—free of charge. Got it?"

Jeff swallowed.

"Now stay here till I tell you to move." He ran out, probably to the next house.

Angry at himself for having charged into a house and murderously mad at Ryder for behaving as if he was Benedict Arnold, Jeff stepped outside. As his eyes looked over the village, searching for a medic, he realized that something was moving that ought to have been still. He stepped behind the doorway, surprised by his calm. A man was stirring on the roof of the nearest house.

The figure was keeping a hand closed around what could have been a grenade. He was ready to throw it at the house that Mort lay in.

Jeff raised the M-1 to eye level as he'd been taught to do, squinted, and squeezed off a shot that ruffled the air near that kraut. The kraut turned involuntarily at the noise, as Jeff had expected. One glimpse of the angry face, and the ragged uniform so filthy that no color could be made out, and he didn't need any other confirmation. He fired to kill.

The German pulled the grenade hand to his throat and squeezed the trigger of his gun hand. Jeff, who had been expecting the last move, ducked back into the shattered home.

Somebody—it could have been Ryder—cursed. Jeff gritted his teeth when he realized he was likely to have another run-in with that hatchet-faced son of a bitch.

Ryder's footsteps were coming towards him as Jeff looked from the man's face to the shirtsleeve rip on his left arm. There wasn't a trace of blood.

In a more careful voice than he'd ever used toward Jeff he asked, "It was you, wasn't it?"

"What if I say it was? Are you going to shoot me? Go to hell ahead, you dumb fuck, and see if I care what you do!"

"You shot that kraut up there? Tell me yes or no."

"Go piss in your helmet."

He couldn't control himself or stop his teeth from chattering as if they had a life of their own. Ryder wasn't pointing the rifle at him, and he supposed shamefully that the knowledge gave him the guts to chew Ryder out.

"Leave me the hell alone, you goddam bag of wind," he snapped at Ryder. "I was trying to save Mort, who's been my buddy. I don't give a German shit what happens to you."

Ryder's jaw twitched with anger, but he didn't speak about that. "Stay back of me."

Ryder went over the next house on his own, but worked slowly and instructed Jeff to watch him. Jeff went into the next one by himself when Ryder said that it was okay for him to try it. He got the impression that the older man was controlling his impatience to know the outcome.

Sergeant O'Caffie directed most of the squad members to help the villagers straighten up their homes and was himself thanked by one of the village elders, a man with hardly a tooth in his head.

Ryder, who wouldn't leave Jeff's side, translated as much of it as he could make out.

"Says that the Nazis have been 'taxing' the villagers out of existence, and using punishment details into the bargain."

The line medic had already attended to Mort, who'd be able to walk but might have some trouble at the base hospital. Under O'Caffie's direction, the survivors of the platoon started a systematic search for any traces of German weapons. Ryder insisted on keeping in front of Jeff to watch for possible land mines. He hadn't thanked Jeff for saving his life and probably never would, let alone formally apologize for his conduct of a little while ago.

"Hot as hell, kid," Ryder said while Jeff turned over a rock in the vain hope of finding a tunnel mouth. He felt as if he'd been hiking for weeks without rest.

"That reminds me," Jeff said, taking a drink. He noticed Ryder's sharp eyes on the canteen and remembered that the man had originally filled it with wine and that O'Caffie had dumped that out.

Jeff extended his own canteen, half-full.

"You'll be sorry, kid. Fair warning." His new friend was probably emptying the canteen's contents into his stomach, but Jeff managed to keep quiet.

"Thanks," Ryder said, giving back the empty canteen. "Let's both of us not get thirsty for awhile."

The only discovery made by anybody in the platoon was a small white so-called fire pill that provided warmth for heating without the use of electricity. Half a dozen were found in one of the abandoned houses.

Sergeant O'Caffie, resting on his haunches near the water well, looked up sourly at Jeff. "The natives are waiting for you, pal, over at the church."

"Why?"

"They're giving that dead Nazi a bang-up funeral and they want you there as a token of respect."

Jeff gaped. "I thought they hated Jerry around here."

"They hate his guts." O'Caffie gestured back of him at the building. "They strangled the mayor of this village and left his body in the basement for a month. Jerry wanted the smell to remind other villagers what happens if they hold out on food and taxes."

"And in spite of that, a Nazi is getting a good send-off?"

"They have some respect for the dead around here."

Ryder said, "These people were occupied for Christ knows how long, but they never really got to know the krauts very well."

O'Caffie shrugged. "Just go over and watch the

planting, and try not to blow your nose or fart while it's going on."

Ryder said, "I'll stick with the kid."

The funeral wasn't crowded, and the ceremonies were quickly dispensed with by Monsieur le curè. Less than a dozen people had seen fit to attend. The body was in a plain casket.

As they stood with lowered heads, the sound of mortar fire rising from the distance, Jeff asked, "Do we sleep here tonight?"

"In this town, yeh. I hope there's some house with a left-over fireplace."

"We won't freeze."

"If it's possible to freeze in France, even in August, we'll find a way. Hell, kid, one thing we haven't got is luck. Hasn't nobody told you that much by now?"

They shared a hulk of somebody's home with five others, all too tired to talk. As Jeff was putting down his blanket, the remains of the door opened on a stubby moustached fellow with a handgun on each hip.

"You're Parton, aren't you?" he asked Jeff. "Jeffrey Parton—new kid?"

"That's right."

"I'm Nils Cardoness—do you know the monicker?"

"Am I supposed to have heard that name before today?"

"Hell, I'm the correspondent, kid. Syndicated to one hundred and forty-eight newspapers in the States. Where do you come from? I'll tell you which local paper runs my column. That is, if I can remember 'em all."

"I guess I've seen some newspaper articles of yours," Jeff said, too tired to know if it was true.

"Tell me something, kid. How does it feel to be blooded?"

"Be *what*?"

"You know, to have made your first kill. You're new at this, so I can get a human-interest piece out of it and let your folks know you're doing good out here. People like me and Ernie Pyle and Dick Tregaskis, we're tryin' to bring the home front closer to the war—you know what I mean? Let the people at home know what you're going through."

"Never mind that."

"Your folks will want to know that you're doing good out here, and so will the people where you come from. Give me your address back home and I'll print that, too—just like Ernie does, you know? Now tell me what it feels like to have killed a German, a Nazi."

"I don't want to talk about it."

"Modest, huh? I tell you, kid, if nothing else I have to admit that I envy you."

"What the hell for?"

"I've been going out on missions and carrying these two guns till my hips drag in the mud, but I never get near one German. To kill, that is."

"You're lucky."

"I want to get my first kill and find out what it feels like."

"You do?" Jeff turned coldly from the war correspondent who was as little like the wonderfully compassionate Ernie Pyle as any human could have been. "Why don't you get your hands chopped off, first?"

4

The lowliest private in the Third Platoon of Baker Company of the Third Battalion of the Sixteenth Army must have found out during the next few days that Ryder had taken Jeff Parton under his wing. As for Jeff, he was beginning to learn more about Ryder even if he didn't actually like him.

Gil Ryder stubbornly believed that he was the best soldier in the army. He took so many chances that the gods showed respect by leaving him alone. Four times he had been promoted to corporal and busted back to PFC, which was apparently his natural level.

As a civilian he had been a racing driver, a steeplejack, and eventually a carnival barker. He hadn't liked the last job because carny shows were on the way out, and all he ever got was an occasional seedy-looking girl and a thin pay envelope.

His father had been an artist who had painted some of the wholesome material that popular buyers loved. He must have done hundreds of portraits of mothers and children, fathers and sons, families, and all that was wholesome and pure.

Ryder, telling Jeff about his father, said, "I'll bet you can guess what happened."

"He disinherited you."

"Aside from that."

It seemed that his father and a woman art buyer had died in a car crash. In his studio the family found preliminary sketches of Hugo Ryder's best known paintings. In one corner, under wraps, they found a series of paintings that would have set a wooden Indian's pulses to racing. Men and women were seen performing acts with each other that might have seemed anatomically impossible beforehand. His work was disowned by those who had bought so many of his paintings in the past, but his new reputation resulted in the purchase of paintings by others and in Hugo Raven becoming a cult figure.

"How did your family like it?"

"My mother figured it was okay."

"And your brother? You mentioned him."

"That was before. He—well, he died before this took place."

"Is something wrong?"

"I might as well give you the whole story." Ryder shrugged. "Nobody I ever met could figure it out."

At fifteen, Ryder had been a nut about military games, moving flocks of wooden soldiers from place to place and re-fighting different battles. He felt as if he was directing the troops, winning where the generals of history had lost.

His only friends had been as nutty about war as he was. If any girl had known her way around military history, he would have been a friend of hers, too. He didn't smoke cigarettes and only drank beer once in a while; all those things seemed to put fuzz on his concentration.

It was Gil's brother who hated the playing with wooden soldiers. Felix Ryder was seventeen and set to graduate High School.

"Why don't you grow up?" Felix snapped at him

once. "You can't play those idiot games your whole life long."

And Gil, who didn't want to get his brother angry, made a joke out of it. "If I can find a business that doesn't interfere with my hobbies I'll go into it—O.K.?"

Gil shrugged it off and went back to re-fighting the Battle of Trenton in the Revolutionary War, and not doing badly, either. Just as he was convincing himself that the results could have been different with only a little more planning, the door burst open on Felix.

"Dammit, why aren't you in school? You're supposed to be taking your S.A.T.'s and not fooling around with this stupidity."

Gil got up to protect the strategic layout, but Felix hit him with a fist and knocked him down. Felix then knocked off most of the soldiers as well and ripped up seven of Gil's war books.

"If I ever catch you playing soldiers again and at your age, I swear I'll go up to the attic and take all your books and rip them up."

Gil told himself that he wasn't sore, nothing like that. He took a long walk—they were living on Leverton Avenue in Baltimore during those years—and then went to sleep. He had a dream unlike any other in his experience. It was World War One, with an artillery barrage attacking the men in a hard-dug trench and among them was Felix. Gil was aware of having held his breath, hoping that the enemy would miss his brother. He had been rewarded.

At one point later in the morning he remembered having been half-awakened by a scream which stopped as soon as he realized he had heard it. He went back to sleep again.

He went downstairs, but stopped at the sight of

Felix sitting with his mother. Felix's face looked almost muddy, like in the dream.

"Anything wrong?"

"I got up in the middle of the night." Felix's voice sounded amost hollow. "I felt like I'd almost died, almost been killed. I felt like—I never felt that way before."

Mother suddenly said, "Studies or no studies, young man, I'm taking your temperature right now."

That was just like his parents, to be very active in trying to help, but without the slightest idea of what might be needed. Gil went to school, hurried out to his part-time job later on, and did his studying at night on the kitchen table while Felix looked in every once in a while to make sure he wasn't enjoying himself.

That night he dreamed, too, a war dream again. It was the Spanish-American War in '98, and Felix was one of the men charging up San Juan Hill and surviving only because of his brother observing and interfering with prayerful wishes.

The next day was no pleasure at all, with Felix looking as if he had been dropped from a high place. Because he was feeling so badly, he seemed more irritable than usual. A shame he couldn't behave better after Gil had dreamt so hard about trying to help. His squalling forced Gil to go to church for once, although he was too edgy to pray for his brother. The words wouldn't come out.

All the same, he had made up his mind to stay awake the next night, getting into bed finally only because Felix complained about hearing him walk up and down. He tried to keep his eyes open. And in no time at all it was the Civil War, with Felix fighting well at Antietam on the Blue side and missing death by inches in a Gray Trap. Gil had hoped he would survive.

It was Felix who couldn't go to school on the next morning, reversing a more-than occasional pattern between the brothers. Father called Dr. Golding, who suggested that all the boy really needed was a change of scene. The doctor wrote some prescription or other.

Felix certainly felt well enough after that day's school to needle his brother mercilessly for not studying harder. Gil didn't argue back. In a way that he had to accept but couldn't begin to understand, the very precision of his knowledge of wars made the dreams so clear and involved Felix with him. He knew in some bone-deep part of his body that he was somehow dragging his brother backwards through every war that America had ever fought. Jeff, listening, said, "That's the craziest thing anybody ever heard of."

True, he had saved Felix each night, but there wasn't any way of knowing if he could keep that up no matter how much he wanted his brother not to get hurt. And he didn't know what he might do to stop it, either. He couldn't talk to anybody at all about what was happening. Who else would believe the evidence of Gil's senses?

He made up his mind not to go to sleep the next night even if he had to wedge toothpicks under his eyelids, as the Boers were supposed to have done with captured British officers. But he had to sleep, of course. Loyal to his own brother though he was, he couldn't find any real way to get out of sleeping.

In the Mexican war, Felix fought at Juarez only to miss extermination by a hair's breadth. The war of 1812 found him in Lewes on the Delaware, being shelled by British ships and again (thank heavens) surviving because of a brother's prayers.

And on that night, with Felix being sick all the time, Gil realized that there was only one war left to fight. He had lost the struggle to keep awake every previous night, but knew he had to win it this time. He had to break the chain, to do what he wanted for his brother's life.

He wouldn't lie down all night and would keep his eyes open. True, he had to jump into bed when Mother came in to say good night, which she still did. He was out of bed immediately afterwards, flicking the radio on. The music bored him. He tried to play games with himself, but didn't succeed. He stood with feet apart and decided that he felt edgy, probably like a sailor off Machias when patriots of Maine captured the British sloop *Margaretta*. No, he wouldn't think about the Revolutionary War. If he did, he might harm his brother.

He decided to open the window, so that he would be too cold to sleep. He was as tired as Ethan Allan's boys must have been at the capture of Crown Point, and again he hated himself for thinking about the Revolutionary War. He had to stop himself for Felix's sake. He nodded, and was sure he wouldn't fall asleep in the cold. . . .

All the same he opened his eyes very wide and they felt stuck together, as if he'd drowned. The first sun rays came through the window. He was grateful. He couldn't have slept, and brushed and dressed himself cheerfully. The house was quiet when he got down to breakfast and was on the last step of the stairs just as Dr. Golding's Chevvy turned in at the house and stopped. Through the kitchen window he saw the doctor hurrying inside. The doctor said a few words, shucked his coat, and hurried up the stairs. Father had been sitting quietly in the kitchen, where Mother rejoined him after letting in the doctor.

Gil heard himself saying, "There couldn't be

anything wrong with—there couldn't be." He felt chilled to the bone, but only in part because of the awful night.

He could guess the worst from Dr. Golding's expressionless face seen at the head of the stairs. A frightened look gleamed in the man's eyes, something that Gil hoped he would never see again in a medical man.

"I'm sorry, but your son is gone."

"H—how did it happen?" Only Gil could speak. Father had already put an arm around Mother.

"I don't know," the doctor said. "His body is colder than natural causes would lead one to expect, and there appears to be considerable swelling in the feet. It's as if he'd been icy for a long time before dying. I know that the windows of his room were closed and the steam was going, but it's almost as if your son had frozen to death."

Gil said weakly, "Valley Forge," and put up a hard hand to his lips.

He himself had hardly slept and had been cold, so it was the cruel Revolutionay War winter of Valley Forge (he knew it!) that had killed Felix as a result. Not, at least, the wounds of war; but hellish damage all the same.

In that moment, Gil knew more of the truth: the juggernaut that had inexplicably started almost in answer to his most secret martial wishes, had resulted at first in his brother's being saved on account of his presence in the dreams. Hadn't he, Gil, known all along that the best hope for Felix to stay safe was for him to hope with all his might for Felix to stay safe? But tonight had been the last of the nights and Gil had withdrawn his help, his presence, making it impossible for him to help. Hadn't he known, too, in some hard-to reach part of his mind, that Felix would somehow be dead on account of his own failure? *Hadn't he known it?*

And for the first time Gil found himself aware of the existence of somebody inside himself who wanted all the things that Gil Ryder wouldn't admit he wanted, an imperious and often welcome devil-may-care presence; even a murdering Gil Ryder who lived and flourished in his own body, his own brain.

Jeff Parton, laying in a blanket in a small house in France and listening, told himself that the little story revealed a hell of a lot more about Gil Ryder than Gil himself probably expected. It certainly had helped to shape Gil into what he was, and in that way was helping shape Jeff and change *his* life.

"What do you think?" Ryder asked, almost anxiously.

And Jeff said the words most likely to reassure the edgy older man, who had asked so many others the same question.

"I think it's a crock of shit."

Ryder gave him a look of what might have been gratitude, then turned over and went to sleep.

Jeff slept badly.

Mort—his last name was Kaplan—had spent a day at the field hospital and his return was greeted with a beer-bust of sorts, and a poker game under the gun in which Ryder won twelve thousand dollars in IOUs that would never be paid off. As for Mort, he had disliked the hospital because everybody lay around in beds and did the same things—reading, writing letters, and talking about the nurses and about sex adventures in the past, as well as projecting new and unlikely ones for the future.

"At eleven o'clock in the night, a girl wakes you up." Mort said. "But it's only so as you can take a sleeping pill."

"Did you want to be the only one who got waked up?"

"I wanted the broad to climb in with me, that's what I wanted."

"If it was part of the service everybody gets, Mort, you wouldn't be happy either."

"Try me out with one of those girls and see how I take to it."

"They're for the brass—you know that."

"Mort, I'll bet you didn't give those nurses any more of a play than the kid would have done. Jeff over here, I mean."

"Sure, I gave them a play."

"What about it, kid?" The BAR man, Granit, asked. "Do you give the broads much of a play?"

"It depends," Jeff began slowly.

"Sure it depends on if you know what broads are for."

Somebody laughed. Ryder sat up to see who was making fun of Jeff.

"I've been with a few women," Jeff said quickly.

"I bet your idea of a wild time is standing a girl to a soda and ordering two straws."

"How *dare* you, sir!" Granit said, raising his voice to a high falsetto.

"I've been to bed with a woman," Jeff said defiantly. "I've gotten laid."

"Yeh, kid? How old was she?"

"Seventeen," Jeff improvised.

"Good shape?"

"Beautiful. Her boobies stuck way out to there and she was hot as hell."

Ryder put in carefully to the others, "If the kid says so, it's true."

Granit, the BAR man, looked a little shamefaced. "I don't want to ride you, kid."

"She wasn't the only one, either," Jeff couldn't resist adding. "There was another kid of fifteen, and that's a real good age."

He was remembering a story that one of his friends back home had told him and would have repeated it as something that had happened to himself; but Mort said reminiscently, "I got my first piece of tail when I was eighteen."

"I got mine when I was twelve," somebody else said.

"Hell, *he* was in there with his mother when he was getting born."

"You take that back! No cracks about my old lady, you son of a bitch, or I'll ream you good!"

"Take it easy, will you?"

Ryder didn't talk about it till next day, at a lull in the day's slogging. "You were real convincing, kid. Yes you were!"

Jeff knew what he meant. "I don't know what I could've said that I didn't."

"It's how you look that tells the truth." Ryder, shining his M-1 with a rag, glanced across at him. "As it was, you got so anxious to cross every *t* and dot every *i* that nobody believed a word you said." Ryder yawned. "Me, I had to fool my friends about it until I was ten years old."

Jeff laughed.

His caution got him into some trouble next morning. It happened when he was on his way to the line for another patrol. Sergeant O'Caffie, who was walking in front of him, turned when he heard footsteps.

"How goes it, kid?"

"Copasettic."

"Ryder been showing you the shortcuts?"

"He sure has."

"If there's anything else you want to know, this might be the time to ask."

Jeff happened to see a tree with a wooden platform built more than halfway up. The thought of anybody standing there made him wince.

"Is that an observation platform up there?"

"The krauts have used it for rappelling practice." O'Caffie's kind eyes suddenly became wary. "Didn't you get any rappelling instructions when you were in basic?"

Jeff was mute, knowing that he had made a mistake.

"You'll get it here," O'Caffie promised grimly. "I want you at this spot at Oh twenty-two hundred hours. On the nose."

Jeff showed up several minutes before the proper time. After one glance at the wooden platform he satisfied himself by looking ahead and waiting for the Sergeant. O'Caffie's determined footsteps sounded shortly. The Sergeant was carrying a length of sturdy rope.

"Okay, kid, how's your head for heights?"

"I never had any trouble yet."

"Then you won't have any this time. See this rope? Take it and do what I say."

In following O'Caffie's instructions, he tied the rope around his waist and passed the balance between his legs. At the waist he made a square knot. O'Caffie then snapped a metal ring to that knot.

"All right, kid. Now follow me."

There was a rope ladder on the other side of the sturdy tree. O'Caffie climbed up to the platform. Jeff hesitated for only a moment. He'd never had trouble with heights, as he'd told the sergeant. At one point he stopped climbing long enough to look down and tell himself that the view was just like an aerial shot in some technicolor movie. Ever since he had been in the army he had noticed that comparing anything to a scene in a movie made that particular thing more real to him—God knew why.

The platform didn't scare him when he stepped gingerly onto it. He couldn't have been more tickled if champagne bubbles had been popping against his nose. The smell of greenery and shells was so new that it was startling.

"Now, kid, you're going to rappel for the first time in your life. It's a gimmick that mountain climbers use, and it'll make life a hell of a lot easier if you have to do some quick scrambling one of these days. In Italy there was so much mountain fighting that we'd all have been in trouble without it, and you never know what's liable to come up next. Just do what I say, kid, and you'll be all right. Come over here."

He was pointing to the very edge of the platform. Jeff swallowed while he moved, stopping several inches short of the point that the platoon sergeant had indicated.

"That'll do for now. Turn around."

"You want me with my back to the edge?"

"Right."

"I won't be able to see where I'm falling."

"You won't get hurt. I'm going to attach this ring to the heavy rope fixed into the tree at the other end. You'll be able to—"

"No." Jeff was surprised to hear himself speaking so firmly. "I'm not going over like a blind man."

"Nothing will happen because you've got perfect control. You can loosen or tighten the rope at will by catching it with your hand behind your back. Make it tight and you'll stop. Nothing can possibly keep you from being as happy as a hog in slops."

Jeff shook his head. "I'm sorry, but I won't do it."

"Maybe you aren't sorry now, but you will be." O'Caffie sighed. "I thought you had the makings of a good man, but I guess I was wrong. Take the ladder down, kid. You've had it."

Jeff climbed down with no difficulty. Back at the line, he resumed patrolling the front along with others of his squad. Ryder pointed out the slight rise where the krauts were practically headquartered, much further away then it looked, and the krauts were dug in so firmly that Boeings and Mustangs hadn't reached them.

The squad's radio man, Sp-4 Avery Varian, was talking about a certain whorehouse on North Park Drive in East St. Louis, when Sergeant O'Caffie appeared. He gestured at Jeff, and Ryder followed with his eyes.

"Kid, you know how to type, don't you?"

"Sure. I said so when I was drafted. What difference does that make now?"

"I've gotten you a break. You'll be reassigned to the typing pool as a typist-file clerk. The work isn't hard, and you only need to fill in on the line when procurement is short of WACs to do the job."

"File clerk?" Jeff looked back at the men he had started considering as new friends. They'd probably make sympathetic remarks when it got around that he was being transferred, but they'd cut him into small pieces behind his back. And they'd be right.

Ryder, who had heard the sergeant talking, came closer. "Did you try for another assignment, kid? A soft spot?"

"No."

O'Caffie said quietly, "Keep out of this, Gil."

"The hell you say! What's the kid done wrong then, if you're bugging him up with a pansy job?"

Jeff asked, "Was it that drill in the afternoon? That business with the rope?" There was a hollow feeling in his stomach.

O'Caffie had turned toward Gil. "I've got no choice with this transfer, Gil. The kid was scared shitless when it came to rappelling."

Jeff had to defend himself. "I didn't want to go over backwards, that's all. I wouldn't have minded doing it frontways."

"You have to do it like the army says, Jeff, or not at all." Ryder consdiered. "I'll bet you scared the wee-wee out of him, Sergeant."

"You know me better than that."

Ryder half-nodded. "It gave Mort a case of near heart failure before he managed it, and he only did that much because Burris Barnes talked him down. What Mort hated was the mechanics of it."

"Mort got the whole business straight, though."

"Let me work with him."

"Gil, there's no point to it. We need men who can obey orders blind, if they're told to. You know the score."

"This kid is all right," Ryder said stubbornly. "Look, I've got some free time coming to me tomorrow afternoon, I hope. Let me work with the kid. I guarantee he'll be okay."

The Sergeant cocked his head. "I have to be there so I can testify he did it. If he does."

"Okay, you'll be on the bottom and I'll be on top with the ki—Jeff, over here. That all right? What about fourteen hundred?"

Ryder didn't mention it until he and Jeff settled in a foxhole for a night's sleep. Stukas were dodging and snarling overhead, making more noise than doing damage. The Germans seemed to have a great fondness for making noise.

"If you can get any sleep with those goddam things upstairs," Ryder said, seeing Jeff lean back, "you can handle the rappelling bit, too."

"I don't see how."

"Ex-lax, kid. I'll take care of you."

It was so miserably hot on the next day that the simple business of moving around made him miserable. After chowtime he talked confidently to Ryder.

"I guess all bets are off today, it's so hot."

"The rappelling? Don't worry, kid, you'll work your ass off."

"My hands will be so wet I won't be able to grab the rope. You can't touch anything on a day like this unless what you want is to get a fistful of sweat."

"I tell you what, kid. We'll take only one chance with it today, and if it doesn't work you'll go back of the lines with the fags and the WACs."

"That's a hell of a compromise."

"O'Caffie has to either get results or break in somebody else. In or out, kid, it's up to you."

Jeff sat down morosely on a rock.

The squad was relieved shortly afterwards, and he soon found himself in front of the durable tree. Crickets chirped fiercely as usual, and mortar blasts from both sides offered undertones to the talk, like music in a movie. A Douglas A-20 flew overhead, almost as if it was skittering in the sky.

O'Caffie was wiping his forehead with a dripping handkerchief when he got there. Ryder whistled under his breath, not caring if the sweatdrops remained on his face. The rope was tied around Jef and a metal ring snapped to the square knot at his waist.

"Up you go," Ryder said.

The climb wasn't as nerve-crunching as Jeff had expected, but his palms were dripping and both hands hurt when he reached the top. Carrying a full field pack didn't make the climb any easier. He was glowering at Ryder as that experienced soldier joined him on the wooden platform more than halfway up the huge tree.

"Now, Jeff, this is going to be easy as hell. Ex-lax, kid."

"Thanks a whole hell of a lot."

"Come over here to the ledge. Look down."

"All right."

"Great view, isn't it?"

"So what?"

"I suppose you wouldn't mind going down frontwards."

"It'd be a cinch."

"Well, you aren't going to," Ryder said finally. "Turn around and face me. Don't give me a hard time, Jeff, or I'll *push* you around."

Ryder looked absolutely capable of starting a tug of war on his precarious perch. Slowly Jeff turned, feeling pressure in the calves of his legs as if two weights were forcing him to stay in place. His arms were heavy.

Ryder attached the snap ring to a long rope. Reaching for it, Jeff felt as if he had put both hands into a pool of mud.

"Nothing's going to be wrong, kid, if you just follow instructions. Left hand on the rope. Now put your right hand behind your back. Grab on to the rope hanging there. If you loosen the grip you'll go down. Tighten it and you'll stop. You can do whatever you need. Got it? Just answer yes or no, kid. Don't tell me the story of your life."

"I've got it, but I can't go over backwards like that, Ryder. Don't you understand?"

"As long as you know what I told you, we're all right. What you have to do next, Jeff, is lay back as far as you can, bend your knees, and kick the hell out as far as you can and slide down."

"Ryder, I don't want to go over backw—"

"Tough shit!"

Ryder ducked swiftly, chopping against Jeff's right kneecap with a hand. The movement forced Jeff to bend. Ryder, at eye level with Jeff and smiling grimly, then put the flat of each hand against Jeff's chest and shoved with all his might.

Jeff let out an oath and started to fall at a speed that was unchecked for the first few feet. He remembered that he could tighten the rope and control his speed. All he had to do was use one hand or the other. Which? The left felt like something scalded by water when he tried to grip the rope with it. The arm nearly popped out of its socket. The right hand did the trick, mercifully. For a moment he stopped himself and glanced down at the view. It was breathtakingly beautiful, a knockout seen the way a bird would see it. All the things that had happened to him in the last few months would be worthwhile if he could only have an experience like this every so often.

The heat had been plaguing him all day, but now it helped break his fall. Instead of letting go of the rope too early his hands seemed glued to it, and he held them in place till the last possible minute. He fell to the ground and rolled halfway over, and when he made sure that the ground was firm underneath he got up.

Sergeant O'Caffie had come around into his field of vision.

"How was it, lad?"

"The damnedest thing!"

"Could you make it again?"

"If you want me to."

"Not scared?"

"I'm careful, but not scared."

"Yes, I think you might work out nicely after all." When he was pleased, O'Caffie's voice took on an Irish lilt that was pleasant to the ear. "You started out bad that time, but you were in control on the way down. Get the pack off and put on fatigues. There's still work to be done."

"In this heat?"

"You didn't enlist so you could laze around all the time, did you?"

"Enlist?" Jeff started to say something nasty and then realized that the sergeant was making a joke with him for the first time. Slowly but surely he was being accepted by these men, all of them.

Ryder was busily cleaning his rifle while Jeff changed. Nobody else was in earshot.

Jeff demanded, "What was the idea, you son of a bitch?"

Ryder grinned up at him. "Want your money back?"

"I want to know why you did that. I could've busted one arm or both or panicked when you threw me over and got myself killed."

"That's true enough."

"Then what made you push me over, you seven-headed son of a bitch?"

"Well, kid," Ryder said thoughtfully, "if you hadn't come out of it all right I'd have known that you can't be depended on in an emergency. It wouldn't be worth my while helping you. I had to find out if you can keep your control when the going gets rough."

"That's some way to find out!"

"If there's anything better, tell me!"

"Son of a bitch," Jeff said again, but there was reluctant admiration in his voice this time.

5

Three letters came for him on Friday, two from his folks and one from his steady girl.

His father had bought a typewriter not long ago and used the so-called Victory model with difficulty. Mr. Parton didn't have much formal education, and spent much time taking courses on vocabulary building or pointing out grammatical errors in advertisements.

His letters recently had been pretty much of a piece. The butcher business was good when meat was available. Mother felt fine except that she worried a lot about Jeff. Was Jeff trying to get a job behind the lines? The local city councilman was a friend of his, and something could be done if Jeff wanted to, for his mother's sake.

Mother's letter was short and in a sprawling hand. Was Jeff all right? He should write and tell them. He should get plenty of rest and eat well. It was possible to catch a miserable cold in hot weather, so he should be careful to avoid it. Please write and tell them everything he could.

Marilyn had sent another picture of herself, in color this time. She was eighteen and blonde, with good-sized headlights—that was what they were called by the boys in Queens. She looked a lot like her mother, which would be a disaster in twenty years.

Marilyn and her mother had moved into the neighborhood after her father died, and Jeff had met her at the local ice cream parlor. Jeff had dropped in because of his father, who was trying to keep from smoking and chewed bubble gum instead. Mr. Parton was ashamed to buy the stuff, so he sent Jeff to do it. Jeff claimed that he was probably the only guy in the whole country who had to buy bubble gum for his father.

The girl at the counter had swivelled her head around slowly and given a girl's version of the up-and-down look. Now that he was closer he could see sky-blue eyes and a pretty little nose that tilted upward at the end.

"My name's Marilyn Ward," she said after a little exploratory talk. "I work as a secretary by day and go to Queens College at night. I want to become a teacher or maybe a guidance counselor. Anything else you want to know?"

By the time they heard straws dredging soda from the bottom of their glasses, Jeff knew he'd found himself a girlfriend. Marilyn folded the straw in half, dropped it into the glass, wiped her lips with a napkin, drank a little water and wiped her lips again. She did it neatly, well aware that she was being watched.

They'd had four weeks together, but Marilyn said that she wanted to know him better before getting very intimate. Jeff accepted that. He was going into the Army soon and wanted to know that there'd be a girl waiting for him at home. He guessed he had persuaded himself that he loved this extra link with home.

Her letter to him was predictable. She hoped he was well and wanted to know what he was doing. She wasn't making any dates because she felt sure that she and Jeff had an understanding.

Jeff held all three letters in a hand. Everybody wanted the same thing. Unburden yourself, they said. Psychoanalyze yourself. Tell your hopes and dreams and feelings. Tell us, Jeff, but don't ask for anything in return.

He wrote neutral-sounding letters to all three, offering bland and meaningless comfort. It was easier to sound like he was on a Boy Scout camping trip than to admit to being scared and worried almost every minute of every hour.

The platoon was returning back to base in dusty old jeeps after a useless patrol when Avery Varian spoke confidentially to him. The small faced and narrow-eyed radioman liked nothing more than convincing other people that he knew their secrets.

"You're in for a real nice surprise, Jeff," the radio man said. "I've had to answer plenty of questions about you, and believe me I gave you a good report."

Jeff grinned. "You can tell whoever it is that I'm definitely turning down the offer to take your place as radioman.

He left Varian open-mouthed and walked back to the squad tent. A sound of mortar fire followed him, but after all this time it meant no more to him than so many bird calls.

Ryder was laying on a blanket and stretching his legs, which were out of boots. His eyes were shut.

"What's up, Jeff? Something biting your ass?"

"Avery Varian says he's been answering questions

about me. Who asked 'em, do you know?"

"The whole fucking squad knows. We've all been asked, not just that jerk Varian."

"By whom?"

"Nils Cardoness."

"That shmuck who thinks he's Ernie Pyle? The correspondent? What for?"

"He didn't tell me and I didn't much want to know. I told him to go roll his hoop. He's a shmuck on wheels all right, that shmuck."

"I'm surprised you don't like him. I figured you and him would get along real good."

"We raise hell a lot, but he—well, he likes being here. He thinks it's a test of his manhood. I can't figure that ay-tall, ay-tall, as O'Caffie says when he's in a good mood. Not ay-tall."

Jeff nodded. He had seen the correspondent, a gun on each hip and a bottle in his back pocket, go out on patrol and come back weary and disgusted because there had been no action. Cardoness had risked death more than once, and sometimes he talked about the First World War, in which he had been an ambulance driver. He cursed more often than any soldier Jeff had ever seen, and admired and envied Ernest Hemingway more than any other human being. He was always willing to drop names, mentioning John Steinbeck at the drop of a hat, and claiming him for a friend. His proudest boast was that he had knocked out a kraut with what he called the ass end of a whiskey bottle, this at Bizerte in Tunis during the early stages of what he called "this test of manhood, this supreme test."

Jeff persisted, "Why would Cardoness ask questions about me?"

"Probably wants to write a story, making you a hero."

"A story? A novel, you mean?"

"No, a news account. He's syndicated."

"I don't need anybody to blow my horn. Next time I see the jerk I'll tell him to lay off."

"That'll only make him write about how modest you are."

"Not when I get finished with him," Jeff said fervently.

As it happened, Nils Cardoness looked him up after chow that night, just when everybody was tired and hoping for a night's sleep without having to get up and attack. Cardoness had been drinking heavily.

"Last time I talked to you, kid, you insulted hell out of me," Cardoness said, rubbing his Hemingway mustache with a thumbnail. "Now I'm going to turn the other cheek, kid. You're going to get the damnedest write-up you ever had."

"Thanks, but I don't want it."

"Listen, as soon as I get to work it's a sure bet things are going to look up for you. I've helped other guys plenty."

"I don't want *you* writing about me." Jeff hadn't intended putting an accent on the *you*, but his words came out that way.

"Kid, you're a damn good story for me and there's no way you can keep me from writing it."

At least Jeff did manage to spare himself any sight of Cardoness over the next few days. The next time he saw the man's name in print it was signed to a news story with two pictures of Jeff, one in the exact center of each column. The photograph on the left showed him wearing civvies.

The news story told about his having killed a German on his first mission. Cardoness had invented quotes from Jeff in which he said that killing was a great test of manhood. In another quote that he had made up Jeff said that his luck was running good.

Jeff noticed Avery Varian studying him enviously as he examined the material, which had been sent by his father with a note to say how proud he was and how his mother was proud but wished he could be doing the same sort of important work behind the lines. Jeff tore it up into very small pieces and noticed Varian's rueful shrug.

Just before he flopped off to sleep he heard Varian saying, "Parton is going to make general any day now, and everybody will be getting him mixed up with Patton. You'll see."

"Is that definite?"

"After the story that Nils Cardoness did on him, the Army would promote Goebbels himself if he was in the U.S. Army."

Somebody else called out, "Hey, General, how does it feel?"

Jeff could hardly keep a straight face. "The first thing I'm going to do is have you guys up on charges."

"Fellows, it's definite," Varian said. "You know I've got my eye to the keyhole, so to speak."

No, you've got your key to the *ass*hole. That's more like it."

"Hey, Parton, you'll owe Nils Cardoness for the one-stripe, if you make PFC."

"I'm not going to owe Nils Cardoness anything," Jeff said firmly.

"Oh, no? What'll you do if the army comes to you with the stripe in one hand and says, 'Take it'? You'll turn it down, huh?"

Mort Kaplan said exultantly, "Kick the cruds in the teeth is what I say, Jeff. Show 'em you're not just a checker piece that can get pushed around when somebody wants to give the push. Turn 'em down if you don't want it."

Ryder growled, "Shut your hole, will you?"

Jeff said firmly, "I'll turn down anything I get through Nils Cardoness."

A couple of men guffawed, which blended in with the sounds of crickets and mortars as Jeff fell asleep.

After a grass-cutting makework detail that the men resented, Sergeant O'Caffie gestured Jeff over to him.

"Avery Varian is saying that you won't take a PFC if it gets offered to you on account of what that shithead of a correspondent wrote."

"He's a blood-crazy bastard, and I wouldn't want him to brag about anything on my account."

"It means a boost of salary and rank. The extra money will do you good if you ever get leave. And who knows—you might get leave in Paris one of these days."

"I wouldn't want any part of it."

"This is like the rappelling business, kid. You have to get some help in spite of yourself. I'm putting your name through for a stripe. You'll come around to it by the time the damn thing is on your sleeve."

Jeff bit his lower lip. "I guess I'm not a very good salesman if I talked you into doing the opposite of what I wanted."

"What you said you wanted." O'Caffie smiled ruefully. "You're okay, kid, for somebody whose parents must be English."

Jeff was briefly distracted. "I didn't think you knew."

"I would have overlooked it altogether if Varian hadn't brought it to my notice. But what the hell, Jeff! We're all in it together. There's another war going on."

Jeff was bending over his bedroll and trying to make up his mind if he wanted to carry a photograph of Rita Hayworth along with him when a messenger came up.

"You're requested to see Lieutenant Liddell right away. When the army says 'requested' it means 'ordered.' "

"I know."

Ryder managed to draw him over to one side and out of the runner's earshot.

"Listen, kid, I don't have to tell you to be cagey with Liddell—or do I?"

"You do. I haven't got the slightest idea what you mean."

"He probably wants to talk about your PFC promotion, and I don't want you getting ass over teakettle into a jam. The lieutenant asked and I said you'd probably behave."

"What business is it of yours?"

"If I hadn't told him you'll be okay, he'd raise some hell with you. He might, anyway, if you don't behave. So don't get smart-ass with the lieutenant."

"I'll do my best to steer away from an argument." Jeff promised. "But I wish to hell you'd kept shut when he asked you. Now I'd get you in trouble, too, if I tell him what I feel. You're a real buddy."

"I knew you'd think so, Jeff."

The lieutenant had set up a table in a khaki tent close to the field hospital. Liddell, who was thirty-five years old and with an imposing manner, could probably have made a latrine seem like an executive office. His hair was thinning and his eyes back of reading glasses looked watery. His nose was pointed and his chin firm; but Jeff didn't think that Liddell had the makings of a leader of men.

"At ease, Parton." As he skimmed through a paper on the table, he paused to glance up at Jeff, then put the paper down neatly, sighed, wiped his glasses, and sat back.

"You've been muttering in your beard that you wouldn't take a one-stripe if it was offered to you. Can you tell me why not?"

"I could, but it isn't easy."

"Maybe I can save you the trouble, then. You killed a man, and don't like the idea of getting decorated for that. Nils Cardoness wrote a story about it and you don't want to owe Nils anything. That's about right, isn't it?"

"Yes. Yes, sir." He changed his mind about Liddell as a leader of men.

"You're not going to hear me say much that's good about Cardoness. Nils thinks that life isn't worth living unless a man is in danger every minute. He's got his uses, though."

Jeff stuck out his chin.

"I suppose you're wondering whether you should dare me to name one use that Cardoness has got. Well, he's famous, and the things he says carry weight on the home front. The army is like any other bureaucracy. It needs all the support it can get and a little extra besides that."

"I can understand that part, sir."

"Cardoness tells people that it's a hard and dirty war, but our men can handle it. That much is the truth. We think it's so important to have it emphasized that our men are able to do the job that we're willing to give him all the leeway that's possible."

Jeff nodded reluctantly.

"Believe me, the bastard isn't typical of war correspondents, but he's certainly got his uses. You're going to get some extra money and status on account of him, and you don't like the idea. Well, I can't say as I blame you altogether, but I'd advise you to take it."

"Even if it's because I killed another human being, sir? Even then?"

"Yes, I think so," Liddell said softly. "I think this is a new kind of war, and if ever a war was justified or killing was justified, this is the one. What the Germans are doing in the countries they've occupied is nothing less than barbaric. It's a throwback to the year one. It's brutal, and their leaders are without conscience, compassion or feeling. They're killing Jews now, but who's to say that they wouldn't kill Protestants next, and then Catholics, and then anybody left with blue eyes or dark hair. In a sense, you are your brother's keeper."

"But that one I killed, he may not have been doing anything like that."

"Maybe not, but he's fighting hard for people who *are* doing that, and who are capable of doing anything at all to further their ends. It's a new kind of war for that reason."

"I think I see, sir."

"And I hope you see that you'll be getting your stripe for having done the most important job of all, and with some intelligence as well. Is it reasonable?"

"Maybe, sir, but I'd also be getting it on account of that article."

"I've had favorable reports on you, Parton, since your first patrol and that was long before Cardoness started researching his article."

"Yes, but the Sergeant didn't say he was putting my name through for a stripe until after that damn article was printed."

"Maybe you misunderstood him, Parton, and the heat's getting to you," Liddell said smoothly. "If you don't have any other questions, then I take it that you're willing to accept a token of the army's esteem."

"I suppose so, sir."

"You'll be held to that, Parton. There'll be a ceremony tomorrow, with photographers and some reporters. The follow-up will be impressive in the New York papers, and Cardoness may give it another play. He's syndicated, don't forget."

"I couldn't possibly forget that, sir."

Jeff found Ryder, Mort Kaplan, and three other men from the squad when he got back to them.

"What's cooking?" Ryder asked. "If you're not escorted by the MP's, it went okay. I knew it would. Leave it to me." He turned to the others. "What were we chinning about? Oh yes, the dinosaurs."

Jeff looked surprised. "I thought there were only two things anybody ever talked about around here, and one of 'em was the war and the other one isn't dinosaurs."

"Well, you're wrong," Mort Kaplan said, annoyed at the suggestion that he was part of a herd.

"Yes, we're cultural as all hell, we are." Ryder grinned. "I haven't got the slightest idea how dinosaurs could 'a done it. If you figure they were built like dogs, well, maybe they did it the same way."

"You mean they went in by the back? That's how baboons do it, too."

"What about ducks?"

"They go in by the back way, too. I think that people are the only mammals who ever face each other when they're doing it."

"What about whales?"

"The back way, too, I'm pretty sure. I once read a book about whales but I didn't know that when I picked it up. I figured it must be a dirty book. It was called *Moby Dick*, but was just about some nut with one leg."

"I once got hold of a book called *The Greek Way*, but it only turned out to be about a bunch of dead Greeks.'"

"The people who put out them books should be arrested for false advertising, if you ask me."

Jeff laughed. "You guys have got your cultural side, that's for sure.

They all laughed, except Mort.

Jeff didn't get to talk to Ryder about his change of heart in taking the promotion. After chow, the company was taken to a theatre to see a movie called *This is the Army*. It made everybody bust a button laughing for the wrong reasons.

Next morning, with a little time to themselves, half a dozen guys including Jeff went out for some target practice, shooting just for the hell of it. Jeff scored well any time he had a chance to measure the distance with an eye before spending his bullet. Ryder was good at snap shots, firing from the hip and coming close to the target.

"How the hell do you manage that?" Jeff asked during a lull.

"Kid, I just take it for granted that I'm not going to miss. Try it and see."

Jeff did, but his snap shots weren't any closer. He made up his mind that Ryder was part genius, part idiot. He himself concentrated on measuring distance with the eye and drawing careful aim. He didn't miss too often that way.

After chow, Jeff climbed into his dress uniform.

"The presentation won't take two minutes," Ryder insisted. He and Mort had come back with him, Mort saying he wanted to change a pair of shoes, but he sat without moving while Ryder talked to Jeff. "Avery Varian says there'll be pictures."

"I can't help that," Jeff remarked sullenly. "It's going to need all the self-control I've got to keep from reaming that bastard Cardoness if he so much as opens his yap."

Ryder grinned. "How's for some high class dutch courage?"

I'm not sure how much I can handle."

"Beer? No, you might get a weak bladder. Tell you what. Mort and me managed to get hold of some soft drinks, and maybe that'll be okay. You wouldn't want to find yourself in the officers' quarters with a dry throat, would you?"

The soft drink was called Choc-O, and Ryder insisted on pouring the stuff out of the can and into a tin cup. It tasted rotten, but he had to do the courteous thing and finish. Ryder clapped Jeff on the shoulder in a friendly way.

For the life of him Jeff could never remember afterwards exactly what happened. There was a ceremony of some kind. Flashbulbs clicked. Captain West himself congratulated him. He could remember, though, that he didn't do anything except smile stupidly when he saw Nils Cardoness. There was no reason in the world to blow his top, Jeff decided.

When he tried to sew a stripe on one of his shirts, he realized that he had pricked himself with the needle and was grinning foolishly down at the drop of blood. Carefully he bandaged the finger, then walked to the latrine and stuck the big finger of his right hand as far down his throat as it would go. It took half a minute or so before he threw up. When he finished he was dizzy.

Sergeant O'Caffie and Ryder were deep in conversation, and he joined them just before chow. "You son of a bitch," he said to Ryder, who had looked a little uncomfortably at him. "You poisoned me."

Ryder pursed his lips, glanced up at the weakening sun, and said, "I didn't want you to make any trouble for yourself, Jeff."

"I could have fallen on my face like a goddam drunk," Jeff stormed. "Hell, if you'd given me too much I might have died."

"I figured one table would do the trick."

O'Caffie said carefully, "I'm not sure you did him a favor, or us either when it comes to that."

"What do you mean?"

"Captain West made a little speech at the presentation and said that he'd be giving us another chance at the Germans a little sooner than they had expected, and was glad to see so much courage in the ranks. Courage and to spare, those were his exact words."

When he got back to his quarters that evening, Jeff discovered a wide-awake Ryder drinking out of a cup with silver handles.

"Sorry, Jeff. Sorry for everything. I took a chance and I made my point, but I might've lost you something even more important if we go out faster than we might have done otherwise and you buy some real estate here."

"Or you do."

"Not me, fella."

"Why in hell not? Are you immune, like Superman or something?"

"No, it's not that." Ryder considered his next words with some care. "It's just that I made up my mind a long time ago that I wouldn't be caught dead in France."

6

Captain West had called the platoon leaders of Baker Company to his tent for a briefing. West was a handsome, dapper man in his mid-thirties, a career soldier. His wife and children back in Middleboro, Vermont, hadn't seen him for three months.

"We've had reports of a kraut concentration near the village of Arneville." He pointed on a map, "Our A-20's have tried to knock 'em out, but haven't got anywhere. Point is that the krauts are going forth from there and raising even more hell than you might expect, otherwise."

Lieutenant Liddell, who had joined the briefing, spoke up. "The locals are friendly."

"Sure, but I don't want any firing on them unless we get fire from there. On account of the villagers—whether they're friendly or not."

"In other words, those bastards get the first shot."

"That's it." Captain West had to agree. "The bastards get first shot."

Jeff woke up early next morning, having planned to spend a few minutes at the remains of the nearest church. It had once been Catholic, he was sure, with its rough wooden benches and ornate pews, but God wouldn't mind if he stuck his nose in there.

By the time he was putting his shoes on, Sergeant O'Caffie had stepped into the squad tent and was telling the men to get up fast if they didn't want their heads handed to them. They were to leave at 0600 and the way they were sitting around with their fingers up their holes they'd be lucky to take chow.

Jeff asked the Sergeant, "Can I go over to the church for a few minutes?"

"Trying to copper your bets, kid? Just stick with the men and wait around. Don't give me a hard time."

Jeff sat on his blanket while the men dressed and talked about women in the vague half-light of morning. Nobody talked much during breakfast, either. Ryder gave off an aura of self-confidence even when he was quiet, as Jeff noticed.

In the cold light of near-dawn, a priest in a cassock with a Bible open in front of him, a hand at shoulder level, gestured consolingly to each of the men as they formed a line in single file. Jeff ws going to get at least a little of the spiritual comfort he had wanted. His teeth were gritted. It took a while to realize why the words made no sense, and then he remembered that he was in France. As if he could ever have forgotten, no matter how many Americans were close to him!

It was dark in spite of the season, and Jeff felt sure that it wasn't four in the morning as yet, let alone oh-six-oh-oh. Just another little fairy tale invented by the benevolent army to make every dog-face think he was being treated like a gent.

The ground wasn't what he would have expected from looking at it by day. Instead of being flat, it seemed to slope, and at times it seemed almost mountainous.

He was damn glad he'd messed around with rappelling a while ago, because he was braced for a long fall. Nothing like that ever took place, but he damn well kept expecting it.

The army seemed prepared. It was possible to stumble along with two canteens and a full field pack, hoping there'd be a stopping point soon where it might be possible to dig a foxhole and take a breath; and yet feel at the same time that the big shits were ready for anything that might happen. It was a brand-new feeling to him. For some reason, it reminded him of an occasional fire-drill at Erasmus Hall High School back home, with the kids lined up in double file and giving answers to test questions on the way out and the way back.

A stretch of what seemed like sandy beach led to higher ground, toward which a number of men were already running in a skirmish line. As Jeff started to run with them, M-1 at the ready, he heard Ryder shout, "Haul ass, Jeff! Haul ass now!"

From the high ground came the noise of machine-gun fire. A number of Germans had been waiting until they were close before firing.

Jeff realized that all he knew now was what he had learned in training. All his past life had been wiped out, all his previous experience meant nothing. Like the choppers, like the rifle in hand and the grenades on his helmet, he was an engine of destruction.

Wet sand made the moving difficult, but the men of Baker Company advanced by fire and maneuver, squads leap-frogging over each other, covered by guards in the rear. Some men crawled forward on their bellies, but they moved forward. The men shouted and some got hit and some died, but the men advanced and reached the treeline.

And found that Jerry had gone.

Ryder had been behind Jeff part of the way. There was such a fierce glint in his eyes that Jeff supposed somebody he knew well had just bought himself six feet of real estate out here.

"Move, kid," Ryder growled, " and be careful like never before."

Ahead of him, Jeff could hear Nils Cardoness, the correspondent, complaining, "Whenever I want to get me a German, he melts into the fuckin' ground."

Ryder's eyes probed from right to left while Jeff looked in front and back of them.

"That's smart, kid," Ryder said when he became aware that Jeff was avoiding duplication. "You've got something between your ears and not just empty space."

Jeff felt grateful at having earned approval, but didn't stop the watching long enough to say so.

They came to a clearing. Five men squatted on the ground, each in dirty gray German uniform. Ryder got behind the same tree that Jeff reached, looking out to see some ten others scattering as well.

Somebody—was it Lieutenant Liddell?—called out, using a language that Jeff didn't know.

None of the five men turned around.

Liddell stepped out onto the clearing, helmet pushed back to a point where his thinning sandy hair glowed in the hot sun. He spoke once more, repeating the same words.

One of the men started to turn, but couldn't do it except very slowly. A rifle fired from behind one of the trees. The German grabbed his throat and fell over. Liddell ducked in back of a tree.

The men in the clearing didn't have a chance against the rifle fire. Jeff fired several times without knowing whether or not he had scored any hits.

Sergeant O'Caffie waited till the men were on the ground, most of them face down, then called out, "Ryder, go out there and make sure they've bought it. Parton, go with him."

Jeff followed, watching the hatchet-faced Ryder firing shots into the soldiers' heads.

O'Caffie called out, "Let the kid finish the other two."

Jeff aimed his rifle at the fourth man's temple, shut both eyes tightly and fired. He kept his eyes open when he fired at number five, but didn't look at the man's head.

From the shelter he had swiftly regained, Ryder called back, "Get the two pieces, kid. I've got the others."

Jeff gasped.

"The rifles, you little prick!" Ryder snapped. "Get the rifles."

Jeff did it and ran back to the cluster of trees. Liddell was waiting, eyes moist, sharp nose twitching, lips curled at the corners as if to keep from saying exactly what was on his mind.

Jeff said it instead. "They didn't put up a fight."

"Too tired, maybe."

"They just let us kill 'em, all five of 'em."

"Maybe those boys were finished with war. They'd had enough. They wanted to die."

Jeff said, "And we killed them."

"That's right."

"You wouldn't say that we did good."

"I wouldn't say one way or the other." Liddell was talking carefully, ironing out the truth for himself as well. "They wore the wrong uniforms, dammit! You don't stop and say, 'Will you surrender?' They obviously didn't want to give up. They wanted to stop and didn't care what price they paid. Well, maybe they were snipers, so to hell with them."

"And maybe they were just tired dogfaces," Jeff said. "I guess we'll only know part of the truth."

Ryder said dryly, "Or guess about it, thanks to Part over here."

Jeff realized that he was the one to whom Ryder was referring. He knew, too, that he had hurdled a barrier in achieving a state of good relations with these men. From now on he was going to be known in an affectionately kidding way as "Part." Nobody had ever called him by any but the most obvious nickname before. He had taken another step in gaining coveted acceptance in one of the world's least exclusive clubs.

Nobody was prepared for it when the grenade went off.

It landed just in front of a cluster of man-high hedgerows and could have killed PFC Raymond Armitrade, if Raymond hadn't walked over to lean against a tree and adjust his boots in the vain hope of making them a little more comfortable.

By the time he had collected himself, Lieutenant Liddell had gotten to the scene.

"That kraut must have got away by water," Armitrade said. "He couldn't fly, sir, and there ain't no other way."

He pointed to his left, where a strip of muddy blue water wound its way to the horizon.

At Liddell's command, a BAR man fired into the air and above the water, not stopping until Liddell tapped him urgently on a shoulder.

"Let's get him alive." He looked back awkwardly towad Jeff Parton as he said that. Nothing stirred on the water's surface.

"Search him out."

"On the land, sir?"

"That's where the bugger's got to be if he isn't in the water."

Jeff and Ryder were assigned with Mort Kaplan to go from one point to a designated spot some twenty-five yards off and come back by a different route. Jeff had a question, and Ryder answered before it could be asked.

"I know the way back is longer, Jeff, but only a damn fool takes the same route twice."

Jeff nodded as if he'd known that much all along. He suddenly became rigid.

Ryder snapped, "Come on, Part, move it. Haul ass!"

Jeff couldn't take his eyes from the muddy blue water.

"I guess I'm having a nightmare or something. I could have sworn I just saw a clump of reeds move in the water out there."

"No wind has been coming up," Ryder said swiftly, his eyes following Jeff's. "He could have fired a potato masher and then jumped into the water. He's breathing through a hollowed-out reed, if he's there at all."

Liddell, busily directing a platoon leader to mark out a search area, stopped himself when Ryder spoke loudly.

"Part has spotted him. Parton, that is, sir."

"Where?"

"Under the water and breathing through a reed."

Liddell looked out, then slowly nodded. "Sergeant, assign two men to keep watch on the bastard and try to take him alive unless he makes too much trouble. I've got another notion."

"Sir?"

"The krauts are in force around here, maybe. Where could they be?"

"I don't know."

"They're not welcome as far as the locals are concerned. If I was in that situation I wouldn't want to sit around and worry about betrayal. I'd be out here, in the countryside."

"Close by?"

Ryder said, "Back of all those hedgerows? It's worth looking into. If a few dogfaces can dig a foxhole, a lot of krauts working together could dig out a whole city."

Ryder reached the spot well before Liddell did. The lieutenant cursed, then whirled on Jeff. "Go with that stupid volunteering bastard."

As Jeff moved out, he saw that Ryder was reaching for a grenade. He suddenly hurled it, then flopped down, pressing his face to the earth. Under Jeff the earth shook slightly and for a moment he lost his balance.

Ryder heard him curse, then glanced to one side and nodded, accepting his presence as natural.

"Here's a spot where a few krauts could live for a while." A flurry of noise erupted behind Jeff and out of his sight. "Bastard probably acted up out there in the water when he heard that potato masher going off."

No sounds had come from inside the tunnel. Ryder nodded his satisfaction. "Join me in a constitutional," he said with elaborate courtesy. "We can pay our respects to Adolf if any of his boys are inside."

"Would they live in here?"

"Not much worse than a foxhole."

Ryder stooped down, which was the only way in. Probably it never occurred to Gil Ryder to do anything but go first and take the danger on his shoulders.

Inside were the smells of moist earth and burned powder, rot and leaf mold, woodsmoke and something sour and sickening but sweet, a smell that Jeff couldn't identify.

Ryder could and did. "There's a stiff not far from here."

"Somebody dead?"

"At least one. And there might be a few people alive and with rifles, too. Goddam snipers. Look careful and look good, Part. Careful and good."

The smell of moist earth had given Jeff the notion that he was in a primitive place, but he soon found out how wrong he had been. The hole had been carefully built on two levels, one underwater. The levels were connected by concrete plates that covered trapdoors. There was a room with some medical supplies and another with three cots. A huge room was filled with what looked like sandbags, but Ryder slit one of them and the floor was soon nearly covered with unpolished rice. One room held a half dozen rifles, and the walls were lined with Western style pin-up pictures: Jeff recognized Rita Hayworth, Betty Grable, a Petty girl from Esquire, and a very good photograph of plucky Carole Lombard. Another room bulged at the seams with pamphlets and papers exhorting the Americans to surrender.

"I'll be damned," Jeff said, having first helped make sure that every room but one was deserted. "I never imagined anything like this."

"It's a new wrinkle for me, too," Ryder admitted reluctantly.

Jeff walked to the rear door of this room and looked out at the remaining one. The first thing he saw was a man seated with a rifle under his knees. Almost automatically he raised his own M-1.

"Hold your water." Ryder had come in silently after him. "That's the stiff."

The man's death hadn't been an easy one, as Jeff saw on a closer look. The rifle had been tied under his knees with dirty rope looped around his neck. The expression on the man's face with its distended mouth and wide eyes wasn't one that Jeff was likely to forget.

Ryder pointed to dirt streaks on the rope. "The German jumped up and down on that till his bones snapped."

"Animals," Jeff muttered through his teeth. "Goddam animals."

Like all the other rooms, this one had to be searched. It had probably been used for briefing the animals on their next moves. There was a map of France, with Allied-occupied areas shaped in black. Colored chalks and erasers were lined up at the ledge before a clean blackboard.

As Jeff stood with rifle ready he heard a sound like shuffling. He raised the rifle.

"Shoot to kill," Ryder said. "You might'a known this is the one room where Adolf's boys would hide out."

Jeff moved forward with rifle extended. There'd be plenty of room to shoot in case the German back of that chair made even one move that Jeff didn't like.

He blinked, then he said in a choked voice, "It's a woman."

"Just as dangerous if she's with them," Ryder said

roughly. "Make sure she isn't carrying hardware."

"She couldn't be." Jeff's voice was still taut, but considerably higher.

Ryder sounded calm. "Naked?"

"Uh-huh."

"Bring her out and let your buddy have a look, too."

Jeff gestured with a thumb for the girl to stand up. She shook her head in a frenzy. She was well-formed, but not more than sixteen or seventeen, at a guess.

She was holding on to the chair. Jeff kicked that chair aside with one foot. It tumbled over, exposing the girl to Ryder's gaze. She called out, then put her hands over her breasts and crouched when she saw the look in Ryder's eyes.

"She's no German," Ryder said disgustedly after the girl had spoken two words swiftly and pleadingly. "She's black and blue and looks starved. The Germans have been beating on her."

"We have to bring her out."

"The guys will never believe we didn't play games before getting her away from here."

"Maybe I can do a little something about that," Jeff said.

The dead man had been dressed in a raincoat. For Jeff, taking it off was easier than could ever have seemed possible.

"Nice idea," Ryder said approvingly. "At least she won't be so self-conscious."

She accepted the raincoat gingerly, let out a deep breath, and then put it on.

Ryder raised his voice. "Okay honey, we move."

As he gestured to the hallway the girl cringed again. Ryder would have pulled her by a hand, but the girl put both hands behind her back.

Jeff heard himself saying, "We're not going to hurt you. We're not Germans. You can understand that, can't you? You can hear it from the way we speak, even if you don't hear the individual words."

The girl began to moan in a voice that wasn't so much high and wild as resigned to harshness and pain. Her tones keened of sadness beyond despair.

Jeff wished he was anywhere else in the world. Ryder gritted his teeth.

"There's no sense talking." Ryder walked over till he was directly in front of the girl, then bent and lifted her on a shoulder. The girl's voice rose, but only a little.

Jeff walked right behind Ryder and the girl, still looking from left to right in case he or his friend had missed any Nazis—that was how he thought of them after what he had just seen—on the way in here. The trip out wasn't nearly as long, and Jeff was grateful for that much.

Liddell was waiting, bent over and rubbing his right leg. At their arrival he straightened. When he saw Ryder's cargo, he stepped forwad. He was rolling a cigar between his lips, but took it out and talked gravely to the girl in soft and even tones.

The girl had been emotionally disturbed by being carried out of the cave, and valuable time passed before she was able to say anything at all. Once she started, though, Liddell didn't try to stem the torrent of words. The lieutenant's face grew taut, even as his eyes softened in sympathy.

He repeated the girl's story in what Jeff supposed was a highly edited version. The girl's name was Mai, and her father had been Jewish. He had been captured by the Nazis when all the men in the village were ordered to strip, and he had been castrated, then killed in her sight. Her boy friend had been a teacher in the new schoolhouse, a Nazi sympathizer who was soon shaken out of his complacency.

Mai's mother was driven to suicide, and Mai and her boyfriend were kidnapped and taken out to the cave as soon as the Allied advance was under way.

The boyfriend had been tied up and starved. When Mai tried to feed him surreptitiously, she was beaten, called a "Jew whore," and raped. The Nazis realized that it pained the man to see her treated in that way, and so she was raped repeatedly. The Germans tied him with rifle and rope, and the men took turns jumping up and down on the rope. He begged to be put out of his misery, but Mai was too weak and helpless to do anything. After a few more days he died. Mai was kept in the room with the body. Every so often a German would come into the room, prop open the dead man's sightless eyes, and attack her.

Once a day she was fed half a bowlful of rice, and sometimes bread. She hadn't spoken to anyone for three days.

Liddell said, "See that she's covered and that she gets something to eat. Not too much—in a condition like hers she could get sicker."

He was wiping his face with a handkerchief when he turned away to the men who had brought her out. "What's inside that hole?"

Ryder described the area. Liddell nodded briskly, gesturing for Sergeant O'Caffie to join them.

"I want all the papers and maps out of there and shipped to G.H.Q. Everything else is to be destroyed and the tunnel smashed. It'll take three platoons, I think, to do it quickly."

"Do you want the food destroyed, too?"

"No way of being sure they didn't poison it. With these sniper bastards, how can you tell?"

He looked at Jeff, daring him to make any objection. Still sick to the soul at what he had seen, Jeff was silent.

Jeff and Ryder followed Liddell to where the girl was being treated by a medical corpsman. She had eaten quickly and now sat with wide-open eyes and stared at the American as if it was hard to believe that he wanted to help her.

The medic knew only a few words of French, and his accent made the girl smile wanly. Then she stopped smiling abruptly as if she had no right to be happy.

Liddell kept up his own smile as he looked at the girl and talked to the corpsman. "I could strangle the kraut bastards with bare goddam hands for this."

"She's had a shitty time. She kept blubbering, 'I'm not Jewish, I'm not.' " I know enough French to understand that much."

"If I hadn't already seen so much in this goddam war, I'd bust out crying all over again." The unvaryingly cheerful voice used for Mai's benefit gave Liddell's words a grisly emphasis. "I've got a kid that age in Pearl Harbor, and if anybody did that to her I'd go out of my skull."

"This kid has had it."

"We'll do what we can." He spoke briefly to the girl, then translated her speech.

Jeff said intuitively, "She doesn't want to go."

"I'm trying to tell her that we'll take her back to the village."

"It might be one chance too many," the corpsman said.

"Has to be done," Liddell said. "Do the best you can for her right now, and let's shag the hell out of here."

"Maybe we'll run into some Germans."

"I'd look forward to it."

7

An old crone on the outskirts of the village gave one look at the advancing party and ran into a nearby house.

Liddell, in the advance, spoke to Mai. "That's a friend of her mother's. Doesn't seem to like the kid a hell of a lot or have any feeling for her."

O'Caffie said grimly, "Let's hope that old bag didn't warn the Germans."

"Let's hope she did."

He glanced back of him to make sure that the soldiers were strung out satisfactorily along the dusty gray road in the blazing sun of this August afternoon.

The house opened on the crone again and on an old man walking with a cane. The old man was vigorous for his years, and watery eyes moved up and down along the string of men on the road. At the sight of Mai, his eyes hardened.

Liddell spoke carefully. The old man turned to the girl and spoke harshly to her.

"He says she's a Jewess and nothing but a troublemaker for that reason. He says that the Germans maybe didn't amount to much, but they had the right idea where the Jews are concerned. Old bastard!"

Mort Kaplan, not far behind, said, "I'd like to kill him." He spoke quietly.

"I'll bet he's the joker who turned Mai's boy friend in to the Nazis in the first place," Liddell said, checking the terrain as he spoke. "I want four men to each house and ten for the schoolhouse. Move it, you men! Haul ass right now!"

The old man's right hand rose, but Jeff stepped between him and the girl. The man's voice rose alarmingly. The greenest soldier in the platoon, Jeff himself, realized that any German nearby might be alerted.

Liddell said, "Leave the old bastard alone, and don't muzzle him no matter how much you want to. Others were watching."

Ryder and Jeff went with half a dozen others to search the schoolhouse at the far end of the square. Back of him, Jeff heard machine-gun fire. Ryder was crouched over and running to the side of the closest house for protection. The irregular formation made by the men assigned to the schoolhouse had broken sharply, with every man scattering for shelter.

Ryder had picked the wrong residence, it seemed. Almost as soon as Jeff joined him, a metallic whistle was heard and a grenade destroyed the house.

Ryder had started to move as soon as he heard the whistle-like sound. Jeff, following, felt enough of the blast close up to be deafened for a few moments.

"There it is," Ryder said from his vantage point back of the next house.

Jeff looked out at a two-story cement building with a wire fence around it and a cement walk leading to the front entrance.

Ryder pulled him back. "You want to get your ass reamed?" But he was thoughtful. "I knew there'd be a few of the lice around. After hearing that old bastard I just knew it."

"Is that the only way you knew? I'm curious, Ryder."

"No, that isn't the only way. Truth is that it was quiet, *too* damn quiet."

"What are we going to do about it?"

"Wait around."

"And keep a sharp eye peeled, I suppose."

"Hell, what do *you* think!"

Lieutenant Liddell and his orderly ran into a house in which the lieutenant had heard a scream. In the house, a young woman turned toward them, seeing nothing but the blood-drenched object cradled in her arms. She was crooning to it. With a sick feeling, Liddell became aware that it was a dead baby.

There was no comfort that he could offer, nothing to be said or done.

"Try to get the baby buried, for health reasons."

The orderly said, "I don't think she'll give it up."

"You'll have to keep trying."

The woman's voice was rising in a wail when he walked out into the clear sunshine again. The medical sergeant was hard at work putting bandages on the arm of a private, who was smiling ruefully as he made and unmade a fist.

"I can still handle anything Adolf throws against me," the private insisted. "Even if I can only use one hand to the fullest, I'll be all right."

"We need every man we can get, soldier. I'm glad you're on our team."

"Thank you, sir."

A little way off, he ordered one of the sergeants to make sure that the wounded soldier was forced behind the lines until he was ready to put his life on the line again.

Machine guns stitched their death patterns against one side of the house as Liddell and the sergeant left it. He looked up to see answering fire, and turned to another private who lay on the ground, watching.

"You all right?"

"So far, so good, sir," the soldier said. "That bastard in the schoolhouse! How do we get him out of there?"

"We have to give him time to run out of ammo, and then let the bastard have it."

"I'd like to volunteer to help, sir."

"Can you walk?"

"I—I have to favor my left leg right now, sir."

"That being the case, get to safety and stay there."

"Yes, sir."

"Do you need help?"

"No, sir."

Liddell called out, "O'Caffie, get some men over here to help—"

A bullet whirled that young soldier around where he lay, his mouth gaping open, his eyes glazing over. Liddell could feel the last thread of pulse in his body.

"They've stopped," Jeff said.

"Either Hans is out of ammo up there or he wants to bring us out so he can take some more potshots." Ryder appeared to be keeping an eye out in a number of directions at the same time.

"The sergeant is telling his men to close in," Jeff said, having heard a booming voice of authority.

"Goddam cluck," Ryder muttered. "First thing to do is blow up that goddam school."

"I guess there are orders not to blow it up. Maybe

it's got a sentimental meaning to the people who live here."

"The hell with that!" Ryder was pensive. "You were asking me a while ago why I figured on the worst as soon as we came into this town. There were no children, none at all. Part, if you get into a town by daylight and there are no children around or no sign of 'em, then you can bet your ass something is wrong."

"I'll remember that when we—oh-oh!"

The men advancing on the schoolhouse had been caught in crossfire from Germans hiding back of nearby apple trees. Jeff saw two men drop, tortured looks crossing their tired faces before they died. He fired at the trees and wondered if he was right in thinking that the second outburst wasn't nearly as brisk.

Jeff wheeled on Ryder. "Do we stay here like fuckin' sardines in a can?"

Radioman Avery Varian had acted on Lieutenant Liddell's orders and signalled for reinforcements. He spoke frantically into the microphone, a hand at his rifle in case of trouble.

The individual soldier knew what to do if he went by the book, but sometimes didn't do it. A private named Humphrey suddenly charged the trees from which the deadly fire had been coming, and was cut to pieces. Liddell ordered potato mashers thrown in that direction, but it didn't seem to help.

Ryder had turned to say something to Jeff, when an unshaven German in a soiled gray uniform appeared in back of him. Jeff started to turn, but Ryder had only to look at Jeff's face to decide what he had to do. He stepped backward as he turned, ducked down, and killed the German with his hands. The German called out once. Jeff saw his eyes bulge. He died quickly. Ryder fired a bullet into the man's head, then kicked what was left of the body as far away as he could manage.

Jeff saw Ryder's disposition of the dead German only in fits and starts, while keeping watch for the other disturbances.

Much as he hated it, he couldn't help noticing and even admiring Ryder's thoroughness and care. The man was good at his work.

Because of his alertness he saw a masher come whistling through the air on its way toward them. He called out, then whirled as if to run.

Ryder shouted, "Flop!"

There wasn't any time to do the safest thing. Jeff hit the ground with hands over his head. The masher must have nicked a corner of the schoolhouse roof and been deflected. It came down at a point less than three feet from Jeff, and it stayed there. He realized with a breath of relief that the damn thing was no good.

"Don't touch the bugger," Gil Ryder called. "Just you follow me."

He led the way to the side of the house nearer the school. The trees had been attacked with mashers and bullets, causing a fire that seemed to be moving past the village's end and leaving the schoolhouse alone. As Jeff watched, eyes narrowed, two German soldiers ran out from their hiding place and were cut down.

Ryder said, "As long as he's in that building, he's got height on us."

"Who?"

"Adolf, you shmuck! Who else?"

Mort Kaplan limped over to them. "Stubbed a toe on one of the bum grenades," he explained, breathless. "How long do you think we'll be pinned down?"

"Don't ask me," Ryder snapped, his temper worn. "If you don't like what's happening, tell your congressman!"

In the distance. a German who had been sprawling in dirt suddenly raised a hand to throw a grenade, but became rigid and let the grenade fall. Jeff looked away, sickened at sight of what the exploding grenade did to that German's body.

Ryder suddenly said, "The lieutenant is out."

Liddell was ducking as he ran and sometimes crouching. When German fire was dangerous, he crawled on hands and knees; but always reached the point he had started for.

"Everything all right here?" Assurances soothed him only briefly. He glowered at Mort. "What's the matter with you, Kaplan?"

Ryder said, "Mort likes to get a nice unserious injury in every battle. It gets him to the hospital for a minute or so. This time it's his big toe."

"It'll get you a purple heart."

From a megaphone, a voice called out with a thick accent, "Lay down your arms, Yankees, or you all die. All!"

Ryder fired twice. The voice wasn't heard again.

A German machine gun barked. Liddell gasped and fell. Ryder reached out, being closest, and pulled the lieutenant back to relative safety.

Jeff said, "I'll get the med corpsman."'

"I'm all right," Liddell insisted.

Jeff crawled to the next house, and then to the area

set up as a hospital station. The medic nodded, shrugging because there was no one else to attend to the moment. Hugging one fragile wall after another, the men ran until they got to Liddell. Ryder stood straight while the others hunkered over, as calm as if he was at a cocktail party.

Liddell, stripped to the waist for emergency treatment, turned to Ryder. "Nobody else is here, so listen. I want that building destroyed."

"The school, you mean?"

"Uh-huh. I know what it means to the locals, but I'm not going to have one dogface's life on the line on account of it. Get the word to O'Caffie and the others."

He sighed. "Funny how you can't be sorry for the German."

Jeff said, "That's because he'd kill you if you don't ream him first."

Liddell's eyes opened a little wider. "Is that what you think it is? You think that's all there is to it?"

Ryder had run off. When he was on his way back, Liddell said, "Somebody has to be a decoy."

"A what?"

"To stand up and catch the lightning, but depend on the others to nail the German when he fires out. I think it'll have to be done. Otherwise the guys haven't got a chance in there."

Mort Kaplan said quietly, "I guess that's me." He had looked carefully at Liddell when the lieutenant made those remarks about not feeling sorry for the German soldiers, and now he was on his feet.

When Jeff thought it over a little while later, he was surprised that the operation went off smoothly. There wasn't one solitary hitch. Mort showed himself for as much as two seconds, waving, then ducked back to safety as a bullet winged after him. From a distant point

Jeff heard shouts in two langauages he didn't understand, and then he saw the Germans cut down.

The soldiers hurled grenades while others fired purposefully, breaking windows and heads, destroying, killing. From inside, Germans fired back with deadly aim that cut ranks on the ground. The gun duel lasted three minutes before Liddell arranged for Mort to give an arm signal to Sergeant Summers. The Sergeant wasted valuable time confirming that Liddell had really given the order, then gestured his men to join him in closing in on the few Germans who were left alive.

And now the engagement was in its last phase—that of cleaning up. According to a quick count taken by a hurried Ryder, the Germans had suffered thirty-two dead, six wounded and four prisoners. Four GIs were dead and twenty-one had been punctured in different places.

A flash rain descended, drenching everybody outdoors and dousing the flames that had been started in trying to smoke out the Germans.

Liddell, in one of the houses waiting to be evacuated with the other wounded, said, "Those buggers need soap and coffee—wine, too, I suppose, being French. And they need food."

In another house two German prisoners were being interviewed, one tired older man and a younger who bristled angrily. The younger one said angrily to his colleague, "Don't you know what the Americans do to their prisoners? They'll maim and torture you."

The older one shrugged. "I've been tortured so much already by your Hitler and his Army that I won't know the difference if it does happen—which I doubt."

The younger one shouted, "That's treason! What you've just said is the remark of a traitor and can be punished by a death sentence."

"It isn't treason here," the older one said softly. "Not now."

As the men climbed into their trucks for a return to a base behind the lines, if only for a few days, Jeff saw the medical corpsman helping others to bring out some of the wounded.

"I just wanted to know about Lieutenant Liddell's condition," Jeff said quietly. "Will he be all right?"

"He'll live."

"But will he back in the field?"

The medic turned back to work, giving unnecessary directions at a pitch that grated on the ears.

Jeff asked Ryder, "Why wouldn't he answer?"

"He did."

"But when I asked him if the lieutenant would ever be in the field again, he—oh!"

"You're a slow learner, Part."

The locals were already organizing their own relief program, planning a clean-up, digging irrigation ditches; Jeff could see gestures so plain that no language was necessary. Soldiers were talking quietly about their days' experiences, about friends lost and surviving, about the French and Germans, comparing the Germans to the Japs.

Not until the truck carrying them was under way did it occur to Jeff to ask about the girl, Mai, and what had become of her. Ryder was two seats off, and it was hard to make himself heard above the motor's full-throated roaring. He had to write down the message.

As Ryder looked at it, his eyes seemed to fog over and his lips turned down at the corners. With a thumb he drew an invisible line across his neck.

"A pair of Nazis found the girl and killed her," he said clearly, when the motor quieted down. "At least she lived to see the war going against the Nazis."

One of the soldiers asked, "Are you talking about that naked Jewish girl? The little whore, you mean?"

"She was forced into it," Jeff said rigidly.

"Well now, I got all the sympathy with the Jews—I really have—but I don't know what the hell we're doing over here fighting for them."

Jeff, remembering Lieutenant Liddell's particular expression, said softly, "Is that what you think it's all about and the reason why we're all out here?"

"Mostly, it is, sure. The Jews have got the money and the power, and they got us and everybody else into it."

Ryder looked at the other soldier as if no one else was on the truck. "Do you know what's wrong with you, Harry? You're a dumb asshole, that's what's wrong with you."

8

Toward the end of that day, Mort Kaplan decided to go to the base hospital and let the medics see about his big toe. His limp had become worse since getting back to base.

Ryder offered, "I'll go with you and watch how nice and easy they kick you out."

"A wounded big toe can be dangerous as hell," Mort said. "Gangrene might set in. And there's always phlebitis."

"You've got to have varicose veins before you can get—oh, piss on that noise! Want to come along, Part? This ought to be fun."

"Okay."

"What about you, Anselm?"

Anselm Tarves, a large and dignified black man who worked in the base kitchen, shifted uneasily on a blanket. "No, I don't think so."

"But this guy is a war hero, for Christ's sweet sake! What are you, a Republican or something like that?"

Tarves smiled with exaggerated politeness. "I thank you for the offer, but I'd rather not look in at the hospital right now."

"Suit yourself. Well, come on, Part. We'll get the war hero fixed up."

Mort grumbled, "You guys make fun of me cause I'm accident-prone."

"Sure, sure." In a different tone, Ryder said, "While we're at it we can find out about Liddell. According to Avery Varian, the lieutenant was operated on. It could be we might get some information."

Tarves cleared his throat and said, "Please give the lieutenant my best wishes, if you get to see him—and if he remembers me. Thank you."

"Will do—and you're welcome, Tarves. Don't bother to keep thanking me all the goddam time."

The hospital was a cement building with its ground floor almost smothered in sandbags. There was a waiting room with half a dozen chairs. While Mort was sent inside to see one of the doctors, limping ostentatiously at every step, Ryder and Jeff tried to get some details about Liddell's condition. An orderly directed them to a doctor, a lieutenant, who said that Liddell was unconscious now and sleeping off the after-effects. He'd been conscious for a few minutes after the operation, long enough to write a note.

"Was he in good spirits when you saw him?" Ryder asked.

"Good as you might expect from a man with internal injuries whose army career is washed up as far as active service is concerned." The lieutenant shrugged. "Be damned if I know, soldier."

"Would his nurse have any idea about that?"

"She might, but at this minute she's helping another doctor with a leg amputation, and I don't think she can be bothered."

Ryder thanked the doctor and said, "A lot of careless guys get shot up around here."

"Was Liddell careless because he moved?" Jeff asked. "If he had played it safe, we wouldn't have come over here to ask about him, or go all out the way we do."

"When you're in a war, Part, you think about yourself first, last, and always." Ryder tapped Jeff on a shoulder. "Let's get back to our purple-heart winner."

They found Mort in the anteroom, sitting down and mumbling to himself. A small brown envelope was in his right hand, and a more conventional mailing piece in his left. As Jeff and Ryder joined him, Mort put the brown envelope into a breast pocket and stared down at the other one.

Ryder asked, "Well, what's your story, chum?"

"They gave me aspirins, but said it was nothing."

"Don't tell me somebody wrote you a letter about it. That's something I'll never believe."

"Maybe someone did. Soon as I walked in, I'll be damned if they didn't give me a letter that had been left by Lieutenant Liddell."

"That must be the note he turned out after the operation." Ryder was frowning. "Why in all hell would he write to you? Open it up."

A note and a tiny envelope were inside. Mort read the note aloud. "Mort, here is a special shield for you to wear over your big toe to keep accidents from happening in the future. Liddell."

Eagerly, Mort opened the other envelope. Then his face fell.

The envelope contained one prophylactic.

Ryder and Jeff looked at each other. "I guess he's in good spirits after all," Ryder said finally. "Great spirits, come to think of it."

Then the laughter started. In no time Ryder and Jeff were whooping, unable to control themselves. Mort had to usher them away from the hospital building before some outraged doctor or nurse could come after them. When they were all out of harm's range, Mort joined in the laughter for the first time.

But he didn't laugh as heartily as his friends.

Jeff's father and Marilyn had been writing steadily over the last weeks, but he hadn't been able to bring himself to answer. His father still wanted Jeff to get a behind-the-scenes job and to tell him what it was really like up front nowadays. Marilyn wrote that she had definitely decided against seeing any other man until Jeff came back.

It was Marilyn's letter that stung him into writing. She was trying to get him tied up emotionally, but the relationship between them had never been strong enough to justify that.

He wrote to his father first, saying only that things were all right, but he was with a great bunch of men. About a behind-the-lines job, he said he'd give it a lot of thought in the next few days and then write how he felt about it.

Having told one lie made it easier to tell another. He wrote Marilyn that he appreciated what she was doing for him and that he wanted nothing more than for the two of them to be together on a slow boat to China, and he'd do what he could about that when he got home again.

He paused while sealing the carefully addressed envelope. Again he had told the easy lie because he didn't want to be without a girl back home. He decided to have it out with her if she wrote even one more letter like the last.

Cautious as Jeff was, he simply wasn't in a class with Anselm Tarves when it came to weighing alternatives and measuring out an exact response. The black kitchen man was generally considered a fellow who slept with his eyes open.

Tarves' history in the army had some interest for Avery Varian, and the radioman told enough about it to make Jeff feel that he knew the big quiet man.

Like Jeff himself, Anselm Tarves had come as a replacement. At first he had turned down invitations for a glass of beer and wouldn't let anybody save a spot for him at a movie. He didn't drink and wouldn't let himself even be seen with a soft drink that looked the color of whiskey. He was competent at his job, which he told any Southern questioner was that of softening up the gals who appeared in V.D. movies; and if he wanted to be let alone he could have his way. It was his own choice.

Anse Tarves was himself responsible when there was another unwelcome flurry of interest in him. Lazing around one afternoon, he saw a chance to save Sylvan Watkins' life, and did it, sparing Watkins a painful death in a trap that must have been rigged up by some departing Nazi—a damned animal trap. It was a favor if ever there was one, and the Southern-born Watkins tried to make a buddy out of Tarves. As usual, Anse was polite but didn't give an inch.

He showed some small appreciation one night when Watkins was trying to remember the words and tune to the song, *Confucius Say*. Heaven alone knew what had put the notion into his skull, but Watkins kept humming impossible variations on that one phrase.

"Doesn't anybody remember the damn song?" he finally asked.

Tarves, who did happen to know it, tried to sing—but couldn't give a sense of tempo that was even remotely familiar.

Watkins laughed. "Even worse than I am, Anse. You couldn't carry a tune in a basket."

"I did the best I could," Tarves said with dignity.

The reserve was lost on Sylvan Watkins. "Who ever heard of a colored guy not being able to carry a tune? You're all supposed to sing great, and screw like minks and be happy when you're barefoot, besides."

The stereotype had struck Watkins as being particularly funny because it was so far removed from Anse Tarves. But he stopped laughing very suddenly.

"What in hell is wrong with you, Anse?"

"About as usual. Nothing wrong."

"You need friends around here, even on a kitchen job, instead of chasing 'em away all the time. How come you're so stubborn?"

Tarves smiles softly. "I guess I ain't what you would call very grateful."

"And that's all?"

"Well, let me put it this way. One night you and some buddies are gonna get drunk and decide to go out and kill yourselves a nigger."

Shocked into quiet, Watkins left the black man alone. Like Tarves himself, Watkins became cool and correct, never making a personal remark if he could help it.

Purely by accident, Jeff happened to be near Tarves when a black man from the kitchen company got tanked to the ears. Two of that soldier's friends took him away to sober up, but Tarves walked in the other direction. He seemed more than embarrassed—he seemed deeply ashamed.

Jeff knew about Watkins' curiosity when it came to

Tarves. One time he made the mistake of talking about it with another Southerner close by. Tom Granit, the BAR man who also hailed from the South, smiled and said offhandedly:

"He wants to be the whitest man in the Army, that one."

"What are you talking about?" Watkins wheeled on him.

"By and large, nigras are moody folk," Granit said. "Should one of 'em want nothing more than to get left alone, do it and be thankful."

"You're the one he means when he says that thing about somebody wanting to kill a nigger."

"Me?" Granit was honestly surprised. "I always talk polite to the boy, don't I?"

"He isn't any more of a boy than you are."

Granit brushed that aside. "Wherever you came from, it isn't Mobile. You don't know much about nigras. In the North they just get put away on side streets and penned up like animals. When you went to school I bet your mother told you to stay away from the nigras because they're mean and stupid. The truth is that some nigras are mean and some are stupid, but not all. I bet you hardly ever saw a nigra till you was older, but in my neck of the woods we know what nigras are really like."

" 'Woods' is right." Watkins said. "There are time when you turn my stomach."

"Well, I certainly am not gonna argue with you about one black boy," Granit said easily.

Jeff always considered the BAR man a geniunely good natured guy except when the subject turned to blacks or Jews and he'd make cutting little remarks. Mort Kaplan was so obviously a nice guy that Granit was careful in talking about him.

"If all Jew-boys were like you . . ." he once said to Mort in Jeff's hearing.

Mort laughed and called him to his face "a *farshtunkener* anti-Semite," and changed the subject.

Nobody had ever seen Anselm Tarves laugh.

Jeff could never remember who was the first guy to say that Tarves must be up to something one afternoon at the PX. It was decided to put Avery Varian on the trail.

The bloodhound had to confess in a couple of days that the mystery was beyond him. "Maybe it's got something to do with his college career," Varian said. "He studies engineering by mail, you know. A correspondence course at some New York college."

Tom Granit chuckled at the idea of a black engineer, but didn't say anything when he was challenged.

Watkins owed Nils Cardoness a debt, as it happened, and he told the correspondent that every so often when the kitchen help was free Anselm Tarves would go off somewhere and probably do some studying. Cardoness snorted.

"Is that your idea of a big news story—some nigger going to school? Stop the fuckin' presses!"

Watkins froze. "You, too?"

"What 'me too'? What are you talking about?"

"Never mind. Forget the whole thing."

Avery Varian was being needled, though, because he hadn't cleared up the little mystery to everyone's satisfaction. Varian finally worked up nerve enough to follow Anse Tarves, but when the sharp-eyed black man saw Avery, he made a point of sitting down under a tree and doing nothing.

Varian was too mad to lie about his frustrations this time. "I'll be damned if I give up," he told the others.

It was Ryder who suggested, "Use a scope to track him down."

"Hey, that's not a bad idea." Varian was tickled. "I've got a friend in procurement—"

"You would!"

"—and he can get what we need. Next time Tarves runs for the woods I'll track him."

"You're the one who should be a reporter, Avery—not Nils Cardoness."

Varian was as good as his word. Just before chowtime that night he looked up Ryder and found Jeff with him. He was upset and signalled that he wanted to talk in private. Ryder steered them over to a tree that hadn't been alive for years.

"My buddy in procurement couldn't lend me a 'scope, but he used it himself to follow Tarves. You'll never believe what he does."

"Tell me and I'll believe it."

"First he comes out of the kitchen and then he goes back in a little later. He's carrying a box when he leaves. Cardboard. About this wide and this big, eight-by-twenty, let's say. Well, he takes that box and goes into the woods and opens it up and takes out a piece of watermelon and starts to eat it."

"He *what*?"

"As true as I'm standing here, Part, he just sits in the woods on his black ass and eats watermelon."

"Poor guy," Jeff said slowly. "He likes the stuff and he's got some kind of arrangement with a cook. He always works it on a day when we're going to get watermelon at chow time, of course. He refuses it, then, I suppose, because he knows that a liking for it is supposed to be a low-class Negro trait. Jesus! Can you imagine what Tom Granit would say or think, for instance, if he saw Anse eating the stuff? Anse can imagine it and he doesn't like the idea. So he hides out

101

whenever he wants some and can get it."

"But he's hanging himself up over nothing," Ryder protested. "He's behaving like a kid with a secret hiding place, and keeping himself away from guys who might help him sometimes. He's doing any number of childish things just because he doesn't want somebody to think he's like a stereotype."

"He's right," Jeff said. "Whatever things happened to him before he got into the Army make him behave the way he's doing now. He's always going to be a stranger, and the hell of it is that he might be able to help some of us sometimes, somehow."

"But goddam it, Part, it's not my individual fault or yours. The guys around here have never bugged him. Even Tom Granit has never said a word in front of him, and I doubt if Tom ever looked mean at the guy. He thinks we might become his enemies but he hasn't got a single reason for that. Not one goddam reason, I swear."

"I hope␣your're right."

9

Two days after their leave started, Jeff and Ryder went into the town of Jouvement, hitching a ride on a jeep. Ryder told Jeff he was going to give him a chance to—well, Jeff would see for himself. He might not enjoy it the first time, but he'd be damn grateful to Ryder in the future. And he dug Jeff in the ribs while saying so.

Women were washing their clothes in a body of water as the jeep crossed a rickety wooden bridge. The town of Jouvement swarmed with refugees, who had turned it into a boom town, most of them working for the U.S. Army authorities or the British. There was a main street made up of open-front tailor shops, beer joints, barbershops, small restaurants and souvenir shops. Jeff wanted to see a movie, *Dr. Knock*, with Louis Jouvet, which was one of Marilyn's favorites; but was put off when Ryder pointed out brusquely that there weren't any English translations on the bottom of the screen. He couldn't be kept from *The Great Dictator*, and it was appalling to sit with an audience too frightened to laugh at Chaplin's imitations of Hitler and Jack Oakie's take-off on Mussolini. The edgy silence, which even Jeff couldn't bring himself to shatter, told as much about the occupation as an afternoon in a just-liberated village.

Jeff took more time by pausing at one place long enough to have a photograph of Marilyn copied on silk. It was a cheap grade of silk and the picture didn't come out very well.

He had never seen so many beggars as in Jouvement, and felt he had to fight his way past kids asking for money or gum or candy. One kid was nearly run over by a pony cart, but steadied himself and went back to begging. The smell of sour wine was everywhere.

Just beyond the main street, an MP stood guard at a building entrance and checked GI tags. Jeff followed Ryder past the entrance and into a V-shaped compound. Ryder headed for a bar with butts of American cigarettes scattered on the floor. He pointed to a doorway hung with different color strips.

A GI came through that door—a little shamefaced but smiling at the men clustered around the bar.

"How'd it go, pal?" Ryder asked.

"Just fine. When it's your turn, get the girl called Marie-Claire. She's great."

"I'll remember, pal."

The door opened on a girl in a purple dress and nothing under it. Years ago she had been fragile and lovely.

One of the GIs walked away from the bar, toward the girl.

"It's my turn, baby."

She smiled and crooked a finger. The GI disappeared with her behind the door.

Ryder whispered to Jeff, "You look sick, Part."

"That's how I feel."

"What's eating you? Is this dump too rich for your blood?"

"Too poor."

"You expect something better in a town that just got rid of the Germans? Something classier?"

"Anything but this."

"Let's haul ass out of here," Ryder said. "I've heard rumors about another place that's very expensive. Only the top-level Nazis went there for ass. I suppose it's absolutely the best."

The two-story red-brick building showed square clean windows with turned-down blinds. Chimes rippled inside when Ryder pushed the doorbell. A tall girl in a housemaid's dress, white apron, high-heeled shoes and no stockings hurried to answer. Her short curtsey was almost like a little girl's; her smile wasn't.

"Madame Cosette will see you in a moment," she said, stepping to one side.

They were led to the hallway and a couple of wooden chairs. From an adjoining room they could hear a man's voice. An opened door showed a huge room with an imitation fireplace and more than a half dozen soft chairs. A woman of thirty was sitting on one of them. She wore a white dress and tiny white shoes over feet that didn't seem any bigger than dots below exclamation marks.

A tall man, ill-at-ease, was sitting on a chair that faced them. Between his legs was a black leather carrying case about eight by twelve inches with four small silvery legs on the bottom. The leather had rubbed brown over the years. As Jeff watched, that man raised the case to his knees and held it flat down, the crooks of both elbows hugging two edges of it.

"I sized up the maid when I came in," the man said in not-quite-American English. "She isn't good enough."

"I can assure you, sir, that we are here to cater to your whims," Madame Cosette responded. "We want you to be comfortable and happy, but also to be a gentleman. The girls are ladies—every one of them—and most discreet."

"And so are you, I've heard, Miss Cosette."

"Oh, yes," the small woman said. "Now then, the girl you want has to be a blonde, you say. Is that so?"

"A blonde with soft hair. And thin."

Cosette nodded once and reached for a white telephone on the small table next to her. She spoke softly and Jeff couldn't make out the words. Reluctantly he left the door and returned to his seat near Ryder. His palms were sweaty, his throat dry, his lips parched. What surprised him more than anything else was that the place almost looked like a private home.

"Men who have important jobs bring their work with them wherever they go, especially in the Army," Cosette was saying mildly. "But never have I seen a dispatch case like yours. The maid should have taken it from you upon arrival."

"She offered to, but I'm holding on to it."

Jeff heard the door opening on the other side of the room. A girl stood in that doorway, a girl with soft blonde hair falling down to the shoulders. Her house dress looked simple but was probably expensive, and she wore a slip under it.

"Jeannette, dear, I'd like you to meet Mr.—ah, Jones. The two of you . . ."

"No," the man called Jones said suddenly. "That is, she's very pretty, but I wanted somebody not so big. I should have told you before."

He held out a hand, palm down, on a level with the top of the chair.

"About that big."

Cosette smiled up at the girl and waved her off, then picked up the phone again. The next arrival turned out to be small, blonde, flat-chested, and without any makeup. Mr. Jones took one look at her and reached for a handkerchief and started to fan himself.

"The perfume on her simply stinks to high hell," he muttered. "I just can't stand it on a girl who looks like her."

Cosette sighed. "You wouldn't care to reconsider Emilie?"

"I couldn't."

She seemed to make up her mind. "I am truly sorry that we were unable to please you, Mr. Jones. At another time, perhaps, my establishment might be more fortunate."

Mr. Jones got up sadly, then stared down at the small, slim, boyish madame in the snug-fitting white. "*You're* about the shape of girl I want. And the height, too, I expect."

"I do not accept patrons on that basis, Mr. Jones, I fear."

"I'll make it worth your while, Miss Cosette. You must like money damn well, or you wouldn't be in this business."

"True enough, but my taste in money does not coincide with my taste in . . ." Cosette paused. "I take it that you would bring that monstrosity upstairs with you."

"Yes, of course. What's inside, Miss Cosette, is going to be very important to me."

"I admit that I am curious about the carrying case. . . ."

"Then you'll do it, Miss Cosette? Say you will."

The madame tapped the fingers of clasped hands

against the spaces between her knuckles, "Yes, I will indulge my curiosity."

"Fine."

"One point, though not of the greatest importance. My hair coloring is not according to your specifications."

"I'll give in on that, Miss Cosette."

"It may not be necessary," she murmured. "I keep a small but excellent supply of hairpieces. They cannot be told from the real thing."

"Then you'll even be a blonde for me?" Mr. Jones asked happily. "That's super, Cosette. Wonderful."

She was on her feet before he could reach out to help, moving ahead of him. She didn't seem to walk, but glided from one place to another with the sort of childlike air that would make any older man feel weak.

"Come with me, please."

Fixing the carrying case more firmly in his hand, Mr. Jones followed out the other door and up a wide curving staircase. Jeff looked up and to the right at a balcony with a number of closed doors and one or two abstract paintings on the walls. Cosette stopped in front of the third door on the left. Jeff and Ryder, looking up at the balcony, saw her open that door and stand to one side.

He began, "I want you to . . ."

Jeff couldn't hear more, but saw Cosette nod and take the black carrying case into another room.

Jeff asked quietly, "What in hell do you suppose is going on?"

Ryder declined to admit that he didn't have the slightest idea, either. "Let's go in here and wait," he said, gesturing Jeff toward the big room. "After all, we're next."

"Okay."

"I know somebody who shot a month's pay on this place. The room is big and clean, with a double bed and a box of candy and a bottle of wine on the night table. Beds, too, with sheets and pillowcases fresh as paint. There was a dinky little rug at the side of the bed so you wouldn't get your feet cold when you got out."

"Was the girl clean? That's the important thing."

"It's not the most important thing, believe it or not. With sulfa drugs and all, you can survive a dose and screw for years afterwards."

"Maybe."

"Even you, kid, careful about everything and chicken way up to here, even you ought to have a pretty good time. This is going to be your first time, and it has to be worth every penny, believe m—what's this?"

There was a piece of blank white paper, serrated at the edges, on the floor beside the chair Mr. Jones had been using. As Ryder bent over to pick it up, Jeff heard a door open on the balcony and went out to see what was taking place.

He wouldn't forget the sight for as long as he lived. Cosette wore a blonde hairpiece, and her skin was chalky white. Her dress was small and blue, with no more material on it than Jeff's GI shirt. She wore thick blue-white stockings, and Jeff would have sworn that she was wearing button shoes. A sky-blue ribbon was set firmly in her hair.

She closed the door in back of her, the door to the room in which the officer who called himself Mr. Jones was waiting.

"Well, I'll be goddamned," Ryder said. He raised the serrated paper in one hard hand and said, "It's blank, so I guess I'll throw it away."

"There could be something on the other side," Jeff said automatically. "A picture, maybe."

There was. It showed a girl of ten or so. She wore a blue dress, cotton stockings, and button shoes. There was a ribbon in her blonde hair. She was smiling awkwardly at the camera. In the corner, a childish hand had printed the words, "Love from Claire to daddy."

Jeff and Ryder looked at each other. Jeff felt sick, and supposed that Ryder was in about the same shape.

It was Ryder, always less inhibited, who said, "I feel like I'm ready to puke."

Jeff nodded slowly.

"I don't think I want to stay. Not after I see some guy who dreams he's making time with his own kid. Maybe I'll be a lot more hard-up in the future, but the muscle is just about gone for now."

Jeff had been hoping he'd find some way to avoid using any of the girls who took money for what they did. If he had known in advance that he'd get his wish in such an unpleasant way, he'd have done anything to keep from going into town.

"Let's dust out of here," Ryder said, "before I really shoot my cookies."

Jeff was a little surprised to hear his buddy take a deep breath when they got outside again.

"If you still want some quiff, there are other places," Ryder stated.

"No. Thanks, no."

The explosion sounded less than a minute later. Jeff automatically covered his face, but Ryder wouldn't take any precautions. He called out, "Wait here, Part."

A number of soldiers had run in the general direction of the explosion, but most were staying as far away as they could manage and hoping to find out what had taken place.

Ryder was back in less than ten minutes. His face was grim, but a wicked glint was in his eyes.

"A delayed action bomb blew up the truck we came in on," he said. "Thank God it was delayed."

"How did it get on there in the first place?"

"It could have been thrown on top while we were riding," Ryder said thoughtfully. "Some goddam guerrilla."

"I suppose so."

"Hell, look at the bright side of it. Nobody got killed, and since we're going to be without transportation for a while we might just as well make another change in plans and meet some of the female population."

"More of Cosette's girls or girls just like them? No, thanks."

"Then if we're going to get back at all, we have to use footpower."

"Walking? Will it be safe?"

"I'll make damn sure of that."

"Let's hope to heaven you aren't bullshitting."

"I've never been wrong yet."

He had been strongly aware of smells all his time in this country, but the current combination of rotted fish, urine, and sickness odors was enough to put off somebody with an iron stomach. Worst of all, as a kind of top layer, was the smell of wine. Jeff didn't suppose he'd ever be able to get drunk again, but hoped in a corner of his mind that he was damn well wrong.

Planes flew overhead, and Ryder paused every so often to wave up at the pilots, who were either Yanks or British. There seemed no Free French pilots at all, and he commented on that.

"The Free French haven't got a damn thing going for 'em except de Gaulle," Ryder said. "That's one frog with a very strong will and he's practically invented an Army and thinks he's sold Roosevelt and Churchill a bill of goods about it. I suppose he'll take over when

France is freed and Laval has been boiled in oil for the goddam collaborator he is."

"War isn't easy to understand."

"Especially one like this, where everybody does the right thing but figures it's a good time to play a little politics, too. Even though the whole world is at stake, and it really is, people are busy building for their futures. You mark my words, the next fight will be with Stalin."

"The Russians? What makes you think so?"

"Well, they want to swallow up everything, and once they do that, it never gets what you'd call unswallowed. Any territory they walk into is never given up, believe me. So I figure we'll be ready to fight them afterwards."

They were walking a little more quickly, Ryder keeping up a comfortable clip. Army trucks passed, but Ryder declined to hitch a lift because he said that everybody would have to justify it later on and make explanations. None of that was worth doing, to hear him tell it.

The man could probably see behind hedgerows, it struck Jeff, when he heard an admiring whistle and saw that Ryder was looking in that direction.

Two girls came into view, each with a well-cared-for dress and very little underneath. Both were dark-haired, small, in their twenties.

Jeff was keeping to the road, but Ryder simply changed direction and walked over to the girls. There was no choice for Jeff but to follow.

"Hi, babes," Ryder said. The girls grinned back at him. "What are nice girls like you doing in a place like this, huh?"

The girls giggled to each other, and one answered throatily. Jeff, feeling like a damn fool, said to his buddy, "Let's get out of here."

"These girls are safe, Part."

"You can't be sure."

"Relax, kid. This is going to be easy."

Jeff seemed to have inadvertently challenged Ryder, which was the last thing he wanted to do. He had to stand by while Ryder tried in vain to get one girl or the other to shake hands with him.

Jeff said, "They won't even look at you."

"That's modesty."

"Sure, kid, you go by yourself. That's a lot safer than two guys going together."

"I don't want to dawdle around here if I don't have to."

"I tell you what, kid: you wait while I take care of 'em both."

One of the girls looked at Jeff in appraisal, but glanced away almost as soon as their eyes met. He guessed that his obvious awkwardness and modesty had drawn her sympathetic attention in a way that Ryder's bumptiousness never could.

He turned and started out by himself. Or at least he though he was alone. At the sound of rushing feet close to him, he turned. It was the girl he had considered the prettier, the one who had looked sympathetically at him.

She said, "Hello."

"*Bon jour.*" He spoke carefully. "*Je m'appelle Jeff.*"

"Hello."

"Can you say Jeff? Try it. Jeff."

She understood what he wanted, and spoke the name as Sheff.

"*Et vous?*" he asked and pointed.

She smiled again.

"Oh Christ, what am I doing?"

When he tried to make up his mind afterward how

it had all happened, he couldn't help feeling confused. He was walking along quickly and the girl was struggling to keep up with him. There was a cluster of trees. Ryder and the other girl were walking some twenty or thirty feet in back of them. So far, so good.

But then it all started happening with lightning speed, all the more surprising because he was ready for an act of war rather than of love.

Ryder's girl suddenly giggled. When Jeff turned around he saw that both the girl and Ryder had disappeared from sight. At that very second the girl with whom he was walking suddenly called out and fell to the earth. Jeff couldn't make out what might have tripped her, but he reached out a hand. Suddenly she was pulling him down next to her. She was smiling, making her voice throaty and soft as she coaxed him to lie down.

Jeff knew he was going to do what the girl wanted, because he wanted it now too. But his usual caution made him point to a cluster of mango trees some ten feet away. The girl nodded, stood up swiftly, and ran with him to the trees. In the shelter Jeff lay with a woman for the first time in his life.

It was awkward and uncomfortable.
But it was good.
It was very good.
It was very, *very* good.
It was wonderful.

He was never sure how much time passed before he heard a jeep in the distance. Reluctantly he looked out from his refuge. Gil Ryder, not having been able to make himself clear in any other way, had run out toward the driver. After a few minutes of talk he turned back and called, "Come over, Jeff, on the double."

Jeff turned apologetically to the girl, but she was looking self-possessed and calm. She couldn't have cared less about what was happening in the sunlight.

He knew she couldn't understand, but he said to her, "I'll come back for you, I promise."

She didn't look up at him.

"*Au revoir*," Jeff said, the words coming out with great difficulty. "So long."

The girl had probably hear that phrase in the past. She nodded and said, "So long, Joe."

It hardly mattered that she didn't speak his name; probably, after what had passed between them, she was too shy.

He turned and ran out along the clearing, and over to the khaki-painted truck with the humming motor. The driver gestured him into the back, next to Ryder, who was grinning.

"Well, Jeff? Have a good time?"

Jeff said sincerely, "She was wonderful."

"I told you that there wasn't going to be the least trouble." Ryder patted himself on the stomach in a congratulatory way. "Come to think of it, if I hadn't stopped for the broads we probably wouldn't have latched on to this truck till we were halfway to the base and in territory that might be troublesome. All in all, a pretty good day's work if you ask me."

"Should I give you a medal now or late?"

"Well, you're not feeling any pain, are you? What the hell, you've had a little recreation and your first piece of ass into the bargain."

"Don't call her that! She was very nice, very

sweet."

"I bet she was."

"The next leave I get I'll be coming back here to find her again if I possibly can."

"Damned if I blame you."

"And this time we're going to have one swell afternoon, and I'll take her for a walk and to a movie if they've got one, and for dinner if there's a decent place around. When we get to know each other, then she's sure to feel better about—well, you know what I mean."

"For Christ's sake, Part, you'll be making me cry in a few more minutes."

"She was a sweet girl, Ryder, and I liked her very much as a person. You wouldn't understand anything like that."

"No, sure I wouldn't. Tell me, have you got your dream girl's address?"

"No, I couldn't—well, it's such a small town that I won't have any trouble. Her name is Claire."

"That's very unusual."

"I'll make it my business to find her again and make everything up to her," Jeff insisted fiercely.

"Well, whatever else you do, keep from marrying the little bum."

"I'll do whatever I feel like."

"For God's sweet sake, Part, don't fall on your nose for that baby. She's just one of the hookers from the first house I took you to, that's all."

"One of the *what*?"

"I wasn't going to tell you, but it's a damned sight better than having you go all goggle-eyed about her. I talked to her and her pal that time when I ran over to see what had happened to the truck. I knew we'd have to walk, and I hired them to service us on the outside and make it look like an accident because you were scared shitless."

"You son of a bitch!" Jeff said fervently.

"I guess your girl is pretty good at that. Her name's Marie, and she's the one who got a recommendation from the GI in that place. I hired her for you. Have to try her myself one of these days."

"You son of a bitch." Jeff said again, but more softly this time.

"Well, Part, you had to learn about women someday."

"Son of a bitch," Jeff said for the third time, and hoped he wasn't going to smile ruefully.

10

He didn't start to realize how much he had learned in the last few weeks until something happened that began in a comical way but didn't end like that.

Baker Company had been on the line for a day and night of pounding rain, and Jeff was beginning to feel that he was a soggy mess. It would have been tolerable if there had been some action to send Jeff and the others slogging around for a few hours. As it was, they had to stand around wrapped in canvas, feeling the clotted raindrops all over them.

Jeff had managed to get some sleep near one of the newly set-up gunpits. As he woke up and turned awkwardly, he saw that it had stopped raining at last. He saw, too, that a green tin jar rolled off his stomach, where somebody had set it down during the night.

Some goddam practical joker, of course.

He shook the jar lightly. There was water inside, and something a little heavier than that inside the water. He removed the cover gingerly, keeping it facing away from him as if he expected some kind of a small explosion. When he looked inside, he winced. A pair of dental plates were swimming there.

He closed the box and got up quickly. Sergeant Green, muttering under his breath, was glowering. Sunlight showed spittle popping onto the sides of his lips. Like most of the others, Jeff didn't have much use for Sergeant Green. He was big, burly, graying, touchy, vain, vengeful, and incorrigibly stupid.

The sergeant would be looking in his direction at any minute, so Jeff decided to take the sudden discovery of the tin box and ask Green about it, even though he was pretty sure whose dental plates were inside.

"Goddam!" he said loudly. "Who in hell belongs to this? Who left it on my blanket?"

He held up the tin box. Green's face became white under his usual tan.

"Give me that!" he mumbled, and started to walk over to Jeff so that he could get hold of it.

The shot distracted both of them, hitting so close to Jeff that he went sprawling, the tin box rolling out of his hands and across the mud. Taken unawares by the sniper bullet, the sergeant had been too concentrated on that tin box to move.

At a signal and a curse, half a dozen rifles barked in answer to the sniper.

Green flopped down, now that it was too late, then crawled on his belly over to where the box had rolled. He opened it, reached inside, then hid his mouth with the back of one palm while inserting plates with the other.

There was a sound of hearty laughter from not far away, and Jeff turned to see Nils Cardoness. The stubby foreign correspondent was on his feet, braving sniper bullets to stand with arms akimbo. He was laughing.

"Sergeant, you're great. Bravest damn thing I've seen in the war. You ought to get a special medal from the American Dental Association."

Green flushed, but didn't make any remark. Jeff, watching the man take such sadistic pleasure in Green's awkwardness, felt sure he knew who the practical joker had been. And he didn't feel sorry for either man.

Green, of course, knew nothing. As soon as his plates were secure, he whirled around to Jeff.

"All right, wiseguy!" he snapped. "Just for that I'm giving you some fresh air."

"I didn't take the box, Sergeant," Jeff began, then blinked rapidly. "What do you mean?"

Green pointed out in the direction from which the shot had come. "There's a sniper in the woods, Parton. Guess who's just volunteered to knock him off?"

Jeff moistened his lips. "You want me to go out there and kill a sniper?"

"You volunteered, Parton. I heard you, and I accept your generous offer."

Jeff was on the point of saying that the Sergeant's revenge was being executed on the wrong man, but realized that no words he spoke could make the slightest difference.

"Do you expect me to go out alone?"

"Nobody else volunteered."

Jeff hadn't heard Ryder, but the man was ten feet from the Sergeant and frowning dangerously. "I'll volunteer to go with Part."

"I can't spare you." Green glowered at him. "You and this jerk kid run together all the time, Ryder, but I want you to keep out of—no, wait. Wait here till I come back. I'm going over to the CP."

Ryder watched the sergeant's bulky form on the way back toward the Command Post.

"Wants an okay from the Vatican in case there's any ruckus later on," Ryder said. "How come you let yourself get caught with that tin box?"

"If I hadn't made a thing out of it, he'd have seen me just the same, and that would've been even worse. I didn't take the damn thing in the first place, you know."

"Who says you did? It was Ernest Hemingway, over there. Just about his mental level, come to think of it."

Nils Cardoness still stood as if he were daring a sniper's bullet to hit him.

"What do you make of a guy like that?" Jeff asked wonderingly. "Not that it matters right now, but he sure is one for the books."

"Maybe we can use him." Ryder raised his voice. "Hey, Cardoness! Come over here."

"Nils to you." The correspondent walked heavily, both feet wide apart, grinning. "You're lucky as hell, kid, being able to go out there alone and see if you've got it."

Ryder said quietly, "The kid might get his ass shot off, and you'll be responsible."

"He don't have to go alone." Cardoness patted the gleaming revolvers at his side. "I can go with him if that's what he wants. If he's too lily-livered—"

"Cardoness, you try to bug this kid up and I'll shoot you in the back before you can get near him. That's a promise."

Cardoness narrowed his eyes dangerously, but kept all remarks to himself and looked away.

Green came stomping back, hitting both fists against his sides in silent anger.

"You're a lucky little shit, Parton," he said, then added, "I'm sending you out there but not alone."

Ryder put in, "Milk of human kindness, eh, Sergeant?"

"Parton, I'm sending you out with Watkins."

Ryder said thinly, "You know I've been helping the kid, and now you purposely—"

"Shut up, Ryder."

Gil Ryder glanced at the sergeant's left sleeve as if to make sure that the stripes were still there.

"You and Watkins will be going around the side and out to the clearing and past it. The reason you're getting help for this stint, Parton, is that if at all possible the CP wants that kraut brought in alive. He might have some information, and here's a good chance to get it."

"Alive!" Ryder's jaw fell. "That's twice as dangerous as search and kill."

"I'll be all right," Jeff said.

"In a pig's ass you will."

He purposely took time to shake Ryder's hand, then turned away. Sylvan Watkins was planted next to an open-front truck a distance away from the line, where he was talking to the driver. At Sylvan Watkins' nod the driver stepped out. Jeff was looking at Gil Ryder.

Sylvan walked off in the other direction, as if he hadn't seen Jeff and certainly wouldn't talk to him. Ryder smiled at his open-mouthed buddy.

"Sylvan didn't see you, and he couldn't start off alone," Ryder said. "I happened to be here, and for the good of the platoon I decided to take his place. There was no time to get in touch with our glorious leader."

"If you go through with this," Jeff couldn't help saying, "Green will put you up on charges."

"Let's get back first and then do our worrying," Ryder said with a fugitive smile. "You don't think I'd walk out on a guy when he needs the best man around, do you, Part?"

Ryder insisted on walking some six feet ahead. No

word had passed between him and Jeff, taking the hard paths, trampling grass, hearing the murmured complaints of colorful birds and the eternal cheep of crickets.

Jeff happened to look out at a patch of clearing and suddenly stopped. Ryder was moving ahead. There wasn't any way to signal him, and Jeff wanted Ryder to see what lay on the ground in the clearing.

He had underestimated Ryder. As soon as Jeff stopped, Ryder walked ten feet and then turned, rifle at the ready, his hatchet face a study in alertness. Jeff gestured him over. Walking slowly, Ryder looked down at the markings on the rich red earth.

Jeff wouldn't have spoken, but Ryder didn't hesitate to talk even though he kept his voice low.

"Hot damn," he said quietly. "I think you've dug the bastard up."

Jeff looked questioningly at his friend.

"Tried to cover his tracks by brushing leaves across it. Maybe in a hurry. Didn't do it good though. A kraut who don't know nature can be pretty stupid."

Jeff wondered where an urban person like Ryder had picked up any natural lore.

"This could be another trap," he whispered.

"Jesus Christ, you're trap-crazy," Ryder said in an almost normal voice. "There's a kraut around here and we'll find him and get him back. That's all we have to do."

"If we can."

"Worrying is no good. Puts hair on your nuts."

"I'm just considering the chances."

"You're just farting through your mouth, Part. Come on and move."

Brushed footprints led to the end of a clearing where the footprints gave out. Grass had been trampled and some other grass pulled out as part of a useless effort by the kraut to hide any remaining sign that he'd been here.

"We've got us a dumbo this time," Ryder said, almost cheerfully.

Ryder was looking hard at a level higher than the ground. He pointed to a stand of waist-high grass, which moved as Jeff looked at it. Jeff's expression showed that he was confused.

"It went against the wind." Ryder lowered his voice so that it was necessary to read his lips. "You go in by one end and I'll take the other. Mask yourself with the other stuff."

Jeff nodded. The grass that Ryder had pointed out was at the base of an irregular triangle. He moved slowly but carefully, trying to keep pace with Ryder, his M-1 at the ready.

Quick as he'd been moving along at his side, Ryder got to the point first. Jeff heard him call, "*Achtung*, you son of a bitch! *Achtung* for Uncle!"

There was the smack of metal against flesh. Jeff charged to the base of the triangle just as a small and tattered boy pitched forward on his face. The boy wore a German uniform and a handkerchief tied over his forehead. The scared face turned toward Jeff, who estimated that the soldier-sniper wasn't a day more than fifteen years old.

"On your feet." Ryder kicked the boy in the left thigh. "*Mach shnell*."

The boy groaned.

Jeff couldn't help saying, "He's just a kid."

"He could kill you, though."

"What with? He hasn't got a gun here."

Jeff looked around.

"First things first!" Ryder snapped. "He's carrying a sticker, for one thing."

"You want me to get it?"

The boy looked from one GI to the other, sensing Jeff's general attitude because he started to smile weakly at him. Rifle at the ready, Jeff gestured down at the boy's knife. The boy nodded eagerly and took the knife out from an improvised pocket between his pants and skin. Then he dropped it to the earth.

Jeff gestured for him to kick it away. The boy did.

Having done what he'd been told earned no kinder treatment from Ryder. The older man prodded him in the back with a rifle, directing him to walk ahead.

Following in back, keeping eyes out for trouble, Jeff managed to avoid watery declines and flies as well. For that much he was grateful.

Ryder was steering the boy toward clearings and actually walking in the boy's footsteps, not taking any chances.

Jeff said quietly, "The kid might get hurt on some trap or other."

"He'll save a GI's life if he does."

"We're supposed to bring him in alive!"

"Only if he's the sniper. You say he didn't have a rifle near him, so maybe he isn't."

It was irritating to hear his own former argument stood on its head against him. "He could be keeping the rifle in a safe place where he can get the base camp in his sights."

"I know he's kraut, but I don't know anything else, officially," Ryder said. "Piss on him."

"He's just a kid."

"Sure, but a kid on the wrong side. Ask him how many GI's he's killed! Go on, ask him."

The prisoner, following Ryder's unspoken instructions, branched off into the short leg of an L in the clearing. There was a low overhang of leaves, and a soft smell that reminded Jeff of honey.

They suddenly heard a screech from the boy. Jeff bent down, automatically on guard. Ryder had taken one look and kept standing, but Jeff glanced at his buddy long enough to see the man's lips grow tight and pale.

At a certain point, a bent tree limb fitted with lethal spikes had risen to its full height and nearly slashed the boy's face into two parts. The boy stood impaled, his blood flowing to the ground.

"He may have set it, and he sure tripped it off," Ryder said. "Piss on him."

"The CP won't like this much."

"That's the CP's ass-ache, not mine. Come on, Part. Don't stand there trying to heave. Haul ass, and you'll feel better."

If Jeff hadn't hesitated and warily kept from looking at the boy, he never would have seen the rubber-tipped metal sheath that was no larger than a finger joint.

Ryder's eyes followed his. Softly he murmured, "I'll be goddamned."

"A bullet, isn't it?"

"From a Mauser or I'll kiss Adolf's ass on Unter den Linden. Somebody fired it to spring the trap on that kid. The trap didn't spring itself."

"Somebody? The real sniper?"

"I guess so. For once, Part, you were right and old Ryder got himself a little screwed. There's some hope for you yet in this creeps' army."

While he talked he had been scouting the ground. "See that clump of trees up there? Shaped like a closed V, I mean."

The trees were on a level above them. Jeff nodded.

"Got it."

"Okay. Now we separate and go the long way around and meet up there."

"And if he fires, I suppose I return it."

"If you've got to freeze him to save yourself, Part, then that's what you do and to hell with what the CP wants."

"I guess so."

Ryder hesitated and then offered one of the few pieces of concrete advice that Jeff was ever to hear from him. "Listen for a slow sound, Part. A slow sound out here means trouble."

Jeff started out at Ryder's signal. It was amazing that he could move so swiftly in no man's land by himself. He had always felt horror at killing bugs, and part of his mind wondered how many had been squashed to death under his big GI boots.

There was an exchange of rifle fire, the sniper's rifle high-pitched and Raven's M-1 offering a throaty answer. He saw no sight of the sniper, only a cluster of trees without any rifle to indicate where the fire could have come from.

He snapped off a shot, and gained some ten feet before there was any answer from the sniper. At least that kruat knew that he was being scissored. It would make his aim less sure.

Then Jeff realized that Ryder had changed tactics. A grenade whistled through the air and dropped across one of the protective cluster of trees. For a split second it didn't seem as if anything would happen, but when the explosion came the tree was reduced to a stump, giving a clear view of part of the inner rim.

Jeff followed Ryder's course, pulling the pin of a grenade off his helmet and throwing it. He had calculated too cautiously so that the grenade was well short of the tree cluster, falling over toward the elephant-high grass that formed a natural fence between the trees and the rest of the world.

It startled the sniper more than anything else that had happened, Jeff was sure. At the moment of impact he saw the man, hands before his face. He had been stealthily leaving the tree cluster. Now he was forced back, his rifle held before him unaimed.

Ryder must have seen the man's movements, too. He did something that Jeff couldn't have made himself do if his own life had depended on it, charging across the clearing in a direct run toward the unbalanced sniper.

Jeff was able to fire two shots, keeping the German from taking aim and looking for a hiding place before Ryder closed in on him. When that happened, Jeff ventured out of his safe place in the brush and ran around to one side, where he'd be able to take the sniper from the rear.

It wasn't necessary. By the time Jeff reached those trees, Ryder was standing over the German, who was flat on the earth. The upturned face belonged to somebody younger than the boy who had died a while ago.

"Did you kill him?" Jeff asked.

"I decided I'd do the CP a favor, after all, and take the little bastard alive. All I did was clunk him with Mike here."

He raised his M-1 a few inches, and then not too gently laid its snout against a side of the young sniper's jaw. The sniper moaned restlessly.

"Up and at 'em, sleeping beauty," Ryder said. "Got to spill your guts to Uncle."

With the business end of the M-1 as a prod, Ryder forced the sniper up. Jeff took the extra rifle, which didn't look like any that he had ever seen.

"*Mach shnell*," Ryder ordered.

Jeff said pensively, "All we've got to worry about now is having Green rack us up on charges."

"You worry too goddam much."

They reached the base perimeter by early evening. The prisoner was taken from them and they were told to report back to their platoon Sergeant. It turned out that O'Caffie was back on the job. The Sergeant cupped his right eye once in a while, a reminder of recent trouble that had kept him out of the line for most of the day—but otherwise he seemed in fine fettle.

"You missed all the fun out there," he said. "Get back into the tent and into fatigues and grab yourself some chow. You'd think that in France we'd be eating a lot better, but it's just the same old GI shit."

"Just one thing, Sergeant, please." With colossal nerve that Jeff couldn't have matched, Ryder asked, "Where can I find Sergeant Green? I owe him an explanation."

O'Caffie's face turned grim as he looked past the barbed wire barrier out to no man's land. A flare rose, lighting treetops and a pie wedge of sky.

"He's at the real estate office," O'Caffie said.

Even Jeff knew what that meant.

"Green bought it?" Ryder looked bemused. "He sent the kid out to get his head handed to him and stayed behind and bought it?"

"He bought it, Ryder, and I don't want to hear anything against him now."

"All right, Sergeant. Green was the salt of the earth and we'll all miss him."

Not till he and Ryder had finished a late chow, which they were lucky to get, did Jeff find out what had happened to Green. The man who told him and Ryder was, of course, Avery Varian.

"Damnedest thing," Varian whispered in the darkness. "Watkins was supposed to keep out of his way, but Green heard that one of his men was on the ass-end of the base and latched on to him. Of course he guessed that you and him had changed places. He started to foam at the mouth, they tell me. Swore he'd find the two of you and put you both up on charges. He'd have cut his grandmother's ears off if it would have gotten the two of you in trouble."

"One sweet character," Ryder said.

"Well, he went around cursing you, Ryder. The sniper was laying some shots into camp, but Green was after you and wouldn't be stopped and didn't care if it was safe to show himself or not. He showed himself once too often."

"So that kid sniper got him, huh?" Ryder sighed. "Any kraut who does me such a favor can't be all bad."

"He hasn't done you no favor," Varian said. "You and Part are going to get your asses chewed out tomorrow on account of him."

"How come?"

"Well, he was questioned and said he didn't have any information about military positions, but his superior did. He acted on orders that his superior might talk and shot him so that a trap sprung on him."

Ryder said, "Part, we saved us the wrong kraut."

Jeff put in calmly, "How were we supposed to know who was wrong and who was right?"

"*You* knew, Part, but I didn't hear you good. It

130

looks to me, kid, like you've just about graduated from Uncle Gil's course on getting along in the Army while you're in France. Wee-wee."

Tom Granit said in his soft Southern voice, "Will you dumb fucks shut the hell up?"

"Yes, massa," Ryder replied, with meekness not meant to fool anybody.

"Remind me in the morning, Ryder, to cut your balls off. Now shut up."

11

It was mid-September when a couple of men in the squad first noticed that Sylvan Watkins was becoming forgetful. He didn't pay up on promised favors, and he'd spend hours without talking to anybody. Mort Kaplan said that Sylvan was getting about as social as one of the blacks who worked the kitchen, Anselm Tarves.

Oddly enough, Anselm was the one man to whom Sylvan did talk. Anselm had resented the intrusion on his own privacy at first, but soon got into the habit of whispering in corners to Sylvan and looking sore if anybody got close enough to hear what they were saying.

The squad was on a makework detail cutting grass near the base perimeter—there had been a series of lulls and the CP was worried that the men might be getting a rest that hadn't been earned—when Ryder said to Avery Varian, "Don't it make you sick not to know what's bugging a certain mutual asshole buddy of ours?"

"All right," Varian said resignedly. "Old Avery does the platoon's dirty work one more time."

On this occasion, Varian wasn't the first to find out anything. Jeff got most of the information instead.

It happened by accident. Watkins hated smoking and generally made a point of taking out cigarettes and shredding them to pieces. If Sylvan was in a good mood, which he generally was, it might be possible to take the cigarettes from him; but as a rule he'd stay in a fine mood but shred the cigarettes to pieces just the same.

When Jeff got up to him in the chow line he saw that the only cup in sight was already filled with torn cigarette papers and tobacco shreds. He swore under his breath, but a glance over his shoulder showed Sylvan already deep in conversation with Anselm Tarves.

The tall black man was murmuring, "Hospitals . . . if your wife is getting . . . . when a friend's wife was . . ."

It surprised Jeff that Watkins had been able to dent Anselm Tarves' attitude of indifference to everybody. He was going to say something, but Watkins looked up and saw him. Anselm stopped talking. Both men waited until Jeff was out of earshot.

Of course Jeff went to Avery Varian and told him that it seemed like something was wrong with Sylvan's wife—that was why Sylvan had been out of everything lately. Varian excused himself long enough to go over to the CP, and was grinning like an idiot when he got back.

"Old Avery did it again," he said proudly. "I've got the story now."

"And you did it without help," Jeff remarked, deadpan.

Avery disregarded that. "Sylvan's wife is going to have a baby and I guess he's worried like any father would be."

Jeff pointed out, "He seems *awful* worried."

"Expectant fathers don't make a hell of a lot of sense," Avery said placidly.

He couldn't resist showing off how much he knew, of course, and made a point of walking over to Sylvan at night to congratulate him on the coming event.

"Guess you'll soon be handing out cigars," he added.

The men close by let out a roar, knowing how much Watkins hated tobacco.

Sylvan turned away. "I hope so," he murmured. "God, I'll even do that if it only works out."

"Is there any reason why it wouldn't?" Varian asked, always wanting information about other people's lives.

Sylvan nodded slowly. "The doctor says that she's very delicate and it's possible that the worse might happen to the kid and to—to—"

A little more softly, Varian asked, "When do you expect the little nipper?"

"This week," Sylvan made a fist. "I'd give anything if I could be there."

Mort Kaplan said quietly, "I don't know if it's any use, but I'll put in a good word with God for you."

"Evelyn can use any help she gets. She's a good person, and it shouldn't work out badly if there's any justice in the world."

"From your mouth to God's ear," Mort said piosly, adding, "It wouldn't hurt any if you hired the best doctors in town, either."

"Her folks have done that."

Gil Ryder put in, "If that's the case, everything possible is being done—so try not to think about it."

Sylvan was getting so shaky as the week wore on that he couldn't take care of even his most simple duties. The men took turns in his place. Jeff pulled a kitchen-policing detail for him and hated every second of it. Ryder drew a leaf-raking detail he had always managed to avoid in the past. When Sergeant O'Caffie saw him at that particular chore he asked some questions and ended up by chewing out the whole squad.

"If it happens again I'll put Watkins up on charges and the rest of you, too," he thundered. "I don't want any futzing off around here, and I want you guys to remember that."

Ryder said, "Tomorrow will be the end of the week, and Watkins ought to get the straight poop by then. Give him another day's peace, and he'll snap out of it."

"You want me to forget Watkins exists, is that the big idea?"

"He's too shot to do anything, Sergeant. We can all see that for ourselves."

"And if nothing comes through by tomorrow? If he's still up in the air, Ryder, what then?"

"We won't pull any more details for him, Sergeant. That's a promise."

O'Caffie considered. "You guys should be called the Bug-up Bastards of Baker Company."

"Have we got an extra day?"

"One and no more."

Saturday came and practically went with no information at all. Ryder told Jeff afterwards that one man after another made some excuse to come over to Sylvan and ask if they could do anything to help. Sylvan told every one of them exactly what he told Ryder and Jeff separately, "Thanks, but there isn't anything."

Baker Company was due to go on the line in the morning, so the men were glum and edgy. Time out there meant being assigned to patrols, handling raids, looking for ambushes. One man preoccupied by something else could cost any number of lives along with his own.

Ryder seemed relaxed, probably figuring that he'd take good care of number one whatever else happened. Varian was surprisingly calm, too, instead of haunting the CP for news he could be first in relaying to Sylvan.

At one point he glanced toward Ryder and suddenly hurried out of the tent, missing the end of a conversation that had held his interest until then.

"If you spend a year without getting laid, the old dong gets shrivelled up."

"The hell you say!"

"It's true. You need to go and get an operation on it, then."

"Boy, I wouldn't let no doctor fool around with my six inches, I tell you that!"

"You would if you had to."

"Well, not any medic around here. They're all right for whatver they have to do in the Army, but not for the real important stuff."

"You'd have to go to London if you were still in the army. A dong like yours, with a hem on it, you got to be very careful about."

"Listen, if I ever got badly wounded, I'd want to go some small place where the doctors really give a damn about you."

'What you want is to get wounded in the best hospital in the world, Mort, where you can be the only patient."

Jeff ventured to say that he was pretty sure the army took fine care of its wounded. Nobody made a sarcastic remark about Jeff's qualifications for offering an opinion about anything except the time of day, and Jeff was grateful for that.

The conversation had been going on for ten minutes when Avery came running back with a telegram. He shouted, "Congratulations, Sylvan! You've got the news and I know what it is."

Sylvan tore it open with fumbling fingers, then sat back and took deep breaths. He looked at Anse Tarves, who happened to be sitting idly nearby, and said, "Evelyn is all right!"

"And the baby?"

"A boy. He's all right, too."

Tarves said, "Kid's a sure bet to be declared 1-A for the next war, I bet."

Mort Kaplan said, "Thank God everything is all right."

Jeff said, "Congratulations."

Sylvan solemnly gave each man a cigar, adding that Tarves had done him a favor and picked them up for him at the PX. Mort said that if Sylvan wanted to be a *mensch* from then on, he wouldn't rip up his ration cigarettes.

Ryder, who hadn't congratulated the new father, thanked him absently for the cigar. Avery, who would generally have been telling everybody what a hard time he'd had getting the news first, was oddly quiet, too.

Jeff didn't know why the two men seemed so embarrassed until the third day on the line. He and Ryder and Sylvan were drying their shirts over a fire in a clearing and Ryder, who had joined them, talked about the efficient way that the Italian women had done GI washing. Sergeant O'Caffie was smililng broadly when he joined them.

"Good news for you, Watkins," he said. The word has just come through that your missus gave birth, and mother and baby are both doing fine."

Sylvan gaped. "What do you mean the word has just come through? I knew about it the night before we came up front."

"Your wife only gave birth three hours ago, Watkins. You couldn't have known." O'Caffie added, "I think the Army did pretty good in getting the news to you so fast. Did I tell you yet, Watkins? It's a girl."

When the Sergeant had gone to check some minor trouble at one of the gunpits, Watkins clenched his fists and said, "Wait till I get me a-hold of Avery Varian, that little son of a bitch. Before I get rid of him, he'll be as white as a turkey before Thanksgiving Day."

"Don't bother," Ryder said casually. "I'm the one who put him up to faking a telegram and getting it to you."

"What the hell!"

"The guys figured you might give 'em a hard time. They're better off without an extra worry, and so are you. Besides, it all worked out."

"Ryder, when bigger bastads get made, you'll be their father."

"All you can blame either me or Avery for is guessing the wrong sex. I wanted you to have a boy. Avery wanted you to have triplets to make the news more exciting. I really had to sit on him so he'd play ball."

"Both of you guys ought to be hung, Ryder—but especially you."

"Well, I was right in doing it, wasn't I?"

Sylvan Watkins asked reasonably, "What in hell difference does that make?"

12

"Any of you guys ever hear of the insult game?" Nils Cardoness asked. "No, you guys wouldn't. You're a bunch of goddam lilies."

It was evening, and rain hammered at the behind-the-lines area without letup. Nobody wanted to leave. Cardoness had come around to one of the impromtu little houses for poker, bringing his own bottle; but now that the game was going against him, the stubby war correspondent broke it up and turned to the others.

"Here's how it works," he said. "You get two guys in a center circle, see, and get 'em to insult each other. Each guy has to answer the other's insult within a given time limit. None of the usual words, though. You've got to be different and original. The one who blows his temper first and charges the other guy loses the game.

"Might be good for a few laughs," somebody said. "Who do we pick?"

It was decided that the two men would have to be friends, but nobody knew why Sylvan Watkins found himself picked as one of the contestants. From then on it was only a matter of time before Anse Tarves was suggested as the second man.

"Better you than somebody who Sylvan doesn't like for real," Nils Cardoness chuckled. He hadn't spoken to the tall black man as many as three times in the past.

139

Ryder, who had been watching Cardoness with narrowed eyes, said, "I don't like this, you two. Get out of it."

"Don't be a bum sport," somebody said. Was it Wheeler?

"If this plays bad, don't you guys come crawling around to blame me or ask how I should get everybody out of it," Ryder said brusquely. "I say it's a rotten deal."

Anse Tarves was scratching his wide forehead when he joined Watkins in center circle, the two men facing each other awkwardly. Their smiles looked more like nervous twitches than anything else.

Nils Cardoness asked Varian and Granit to act as judges, but the Southerner refused. Jeff was drafted into service and joined Nils Cardoness as fellow judge. The way it was finally worked out, an insult had to be answered in ten seconds. Repeats of words wouldn't be allowed. The game was to be played for no longer than ten minutes.

Sylvan Watkins won the chance to start. "You're a pig," he said after a pause.

Cardoness, frowning, held up a chubby hand. "You boys will run through the whole animal kingdom if we let you. From now on, if one man calls the other an animal, the other has got to add something or say something before it, like, 'You son of a pig.' And if you're called that, you can't answer back by calling the other guy a son of a horse. You can see why. It's practically repeating what he said, and it doesn't count."

Cardoness smiled cheerfully when he was finished. Tarves, running a hand down his face, grinned at a flushed Watkins.

"You're an elephant's ear."

"Horse's asshole."

After Sylvan had called his friend a name, he winked.

Anselm Tarves, whose face happened to be long and was considered horselike, looked annoyed. His head shot back, and his bloodless lower lip jutted forward.

"Ape!"

Watkins looked down abruptly at his hairy arms and flushed. "You've got no brains," he said suddenly. "Don't you know these bastards all want to get you sore?"

The men howled. Tarves himself smiled at Watkins after a pause.

"You ought to be committed," he said weakly.

Without any warmth in his voice, Watkins said, "Fag!"

The men laughed and applauded, calling out insults themselves till Cardoness reluctantly ruled against it at Jeff's repeated prodding.

Tarves said, "You and the MP's don't get along so bad, either."

"You look like a cow." Watkins taunted his friend. "Them big brown eyes."

"Baboon! That's what everybody else calls you around here. Watkins the baboon!"

Sylvan's jaw was suddenly as hard as the taut fist he made. He moved a fist forward, but stopped himself and took time unmaking it. A red patch had spread over his face, briefly scarring one cheek.

Ryder said tautly, "Don't you think you goons have had enough fun?"

The others waved their hands at him with palms downward. Ryder didn't quiet down till he saw that Watkins and Tarves had become determined to concentrate on this matter. Most of the men had already put down bets of money or cigarettes or loose tobacco. Nils Cardoness, glancing eagerly from Watkins to Tarves, eyes slitted, face flushed with what only Ryder and perhaps Jeff recognized as pure malicious pleasure, took a deep breath.

Loudly Tarves cried, "Pimp!"

"Liar!"

"Jackass!"

"You're gutless," Watkins, now. "That's what's wrong with you. When there's something you don't like or want, you turn your back on it."

Tarves gestured feebly. "That's a fairy tale and you know it."

"The hell it is! You're a coward and that's all there is to it. Scared of your own shadow. No wonder you're in a kitchen detail. That's all you're good for."

Jeff realized that Ryder was signalling urgently for him to stop this in any possible way. "Time's up and it's a draw," he said.

Nils Cardoness snapped, "There's plenty of time, you! Shut the fuck up!"

Ryder said softly, "Watch it, Nils! Your meanness is showing."

The men were quieter now, not enjoying themselves but not keyed up either. Jake Oldham, who was studying for a high school diploma during his spare time, opened a textbook and turned his back on the others.

Rain had stopped with surprising suddenness. Cardoness reached for the wide-mouthed whisky bottle he had brought along.

"I'm going to grab me some shut-eye." He was murmuring under his breath about guys who can't take a joke, and stepped out of the tent as if pacing the deck of a ship against high wind.

Ryder said, "That bastard out there has done

enough damage for one night."

He glanced from Tarves to Watkins as he spoke. Jeff, his eyes following, saw the men's muted sullen expressions and found himself in complete agreement.

Jeff was rooting around in back of his bedding roll when Watkins walked out a little afterwards, and was talking to Mort Kaplan about something trivial when Anse Tarves left.

He wheeled around on Ryder. "Those two got damned pissed off at each other, and they're likely to want to get even, now there's no immediate pressure on us."

"Not a chance." Ryder turned over on his bedding roll.

"And because you doubt it, that's the last word, I suppose," Jeff said with unusual nastiness.

"That's the trouble with something like the insult game," Ryder said comfortably. "A spectator gets carried away and starts it on his own."

Mort Kaplan was halfway to the jerry-built door when Jeff looked up to find out first-hand if anything else had gone cockeyed.

"No sign of 'em."

"*What*? Where in hell did they go?"

Ryder said with certainty, "They went after that malicious bastard who started this whole thing. They might be sore at each other, but they both hate Cardoness."

"Our own Ernie Pyle," Mort Kaplan said quietly. "Cardoness, of course."

"Don't you think we ought to break it up?"

"Maybe." Ryder looked at his watch. "They've had a few minutes, and they're both strong enough to have done some damage in that time."

Ryder reached the door first, even though he had

been at the farthest end when he started. The night was moonless except for a sliver that looked like something off a fingernail.

Jeff waited till the men had run off, then decided that no sound was coming from any direction as far as he could tell, and figured that he might just as well join the others after all.

A tree stump nearly tripped him as he ran. The closer he came to Ryder and Oldham, the more clearly he could hear curses and shouts. There was a sound like a melon being split open.

By the time he himself got to the men, seven of them were making a rough circle around Sylvan Watkins, Anselm Tarves and a corpse.

Nobody could look at Nils Cardoness and think that any life clung to him. The back of his neck had cracked across another of those tree stumps, and he was staring sightlessly at the sky.

Watkins said heavily, "His own fault."

There wasn't any tone whatever in Gil Ryder's voice. "We saw what happened."

"Then you know it was his own fault."

"Uh-huh. We all heard him shouting that he wanted to rip the coon to pieces. He made a grab for Anse and then cracked the bottle against that stump and came at Anse with the glass held out as a weapon. Anse stood there and waited for him to get closer."

Anse Tarves couldn't help putting in, "Some coward, huh? Some coward."

Jeff gritted his teeth. The black man was still remembering his friend's accusation during that so-called game.

"Then Sylvan hit him in the side. He fell over the broken glass of the bottle and tumbled, hitting the back of his neck against the stump."

"I didn't want him to think I was out of Anse's corner," Sylvan Watkins said.

Tarves remarked bitterly, "You guessed I'd turn tail and run like hell away from a white man. You say you're a friend of mine, but you still think I need to have somebody like you to take care of my fighting for me. Well, you can get that idea out of your head for good, starting right now."

"Forget that stuff," Ryder said brusquely before Watkins could offer any response. "Every one of us except Jeff, who came too late, saw what happened and is willing to say so. Anybody who won't talk up for Anse and Sylvan here had better talk up right now and give his reasons."

Tom Granit, the Southerner, asked softly, "Is that there question aimed at me, Gil?"

"It's being aimed, period. If you want to catch it, go right to hell ahead."

"I saw what happened, which is what you say, and I'll tell anybody who asks me just exactly what I saw."

"Then I take it we're all agreed? Swell. In that case, we'd better let the army in on it. Jeff, hop over to the CP and tell 'em there's been—uh—a bad accident."

Jeff had seen so little of what happened at the place where Cardoness died that he wasn't called on to give testimony at the court-style proceeding that took place next day in one of the admin buildings. For the first time in his army career, Jeff saw a general up close and saw Major West take second place to another man.

The soldiers who did testify told Jeff about being led into the room where half a dozen members of the army brass heard what they had to say and asked some questions and let them go. Sylvan Watkins and Anse Tarves were treated like the rest of them and not as if they were the one who had caused the damage.

Sergeant O'Caffie told the men that night to hurry over to see Lieutenant Hearn, who had taken Liddell's place and was in possession of the desk the other man had used. Tall and crew-cut and maybe twenty-five years old, Hearn was riffling through papers when the platoon members came in and stood at attention.

"At ease, all of you!" Hearn hadn't looked up. "You guys really gave the U.S. Army the old finger today, didn't you?"

No one responded to that, not even the hard-to-control Gil Ryder.

Hearn leaned forward. "Now hear me good, you men, all of you. Nils Cardoness was a war correspondent, no Ernie Pyle or Ray Clapper or Dick Tregaskis, but somebody the army could work with. He glorified the fighting man and he was a friend to all soldiers. That's gospel I'm giving you guys, the revealed word. Anybody snickers, and I shoot all your asses off. Is there some comment?"

"Yes, sir." Ryder picked his words carefully. "Nils Cardoness was a mean stupid son of a bitch who kept yelling loud and clear that he was never afraid of anything. He yelled it so loud and clear that everybody must have known he was scared shitless of birds in the trees or anything else. He was no good, sir."

"Anything else? Some more pearls of wisdom?"

"I think I've shot my wad, sir."

"Anybody else?"

Jeff started to make it clear how much he agreed

with Ryder's sentiments, but became aware of Ryder gesturing him to silence. Ryder's eyes were glinting, and a smile had started up at the corners of his lips.

"No contradictions to that," Hearn said, looking from one face to the next. "I get the message, and I'm sure the Army got it after today."

The silence was complete.

"Because Nils Cardoness was so universally respected and beloved by the GI's he glorified, you ungrateful bastards will be sorry to hear that he died."

Only Mort Kaplan ventured on a mild joke. "He was like a member of the family."

"That tells us as much about your family as we could possibly want to know." Lieutenant Hearn nodded. "Nils Cardoness will be shipped back to the States with all the publicity the Army can get for him, and he'll be buried in a GI cemetery, which is what he wanted so he could be close to his beloved GIs. When I use the word 'beloved,' of course, I don't mean anything disrespectful to the memory or the masculinity of the man who was a friend of every U.S. fighting man. All clear, you ungrateful pisspots?"

Ryder spoke for them all. "Perfectly clear, sir. Can I ask how our friend died?"

"As a result of sniper fire, which is what he would have wanted. You might say that he died in action, or as close to it as he got. A sniper has been plaguing the base recently, and he killed two other men before he was himself destroyed."

Ryder said carefully, "I didn't realize there was a bullet hole in his body when I saw it."

"There's a bullet hole in Nils' forehead," Hearn said easily. "It was made by a bullet from the gun we took away from the sniper, a Mauser. Just in case of need there are pictures to prove which gun that bullet came from. Do you pisspots read me?"

"Perfectly, Sir."

"Good. Just remember one more thing: the army never screws up. Only soldiers do."

"Yes, sir."

"Now I know that you men are prostrated by grief on account of what happened to your close friend. Besides that, you've been on the line for a long time. You're overdue for a little compassionate leave until this whole incident blows over. I think that a week should be enough."

"Thank you, sir." Ryder took it on himself to talk for his stunned squad mates. "We'll be mourning Nils all the time."

Lieutenant Hearn stood up to take their salute and return it. Jeff realized that the lieutenant hadn't cracked a smile during the interview and found himself thinking that it was possible he might get to like Lieutenant Liddell's successor.

When they left, Avery Varian turned to Ryder and said, "I'll bet they really line us up for a bitch of a job when we get back. Otherwise they'd never give us a good leave like that."

Ryder shrugged.

"Don't you care a damn?"

"Sure I do, but no matter what the army comes up with, you can bet your last franc, *mon brave*, that Uncle Gil is going to take real good care of himself."

"And take care of Part, too, I suppose."

"Private Parton can take very good care of himself now."

Jeff and Ryder were able to hitch a ride into the town of Saint Auban. They were on the jeep when Ryder turned to Jeff. "You know what's so strange about that whole business?"

"Cardoness' buying it, you mean?"

"He started the whole insult game business to drive a black guy and a white guy away from each other, but he made his point."

"Watkins and Tarves won't talk to each other." Ryder agreed. "And Tarves doesn't talk to anybody unless it's necessary. Your friend, Mr. Cardoness, drove that poor black boob right back into his shell."

"Is that all you can say about it?"

"Well, Part, if you ever get a little older, you'll realize that in the Army you can't do anything about what you can't help. If a guy wants nothing to do with you, then you let him alone. If two guys want nothing to do with each other, then you let the two of 'em alone. Got a chocolate bar on you?"

"My last one."

"Thanks, Part. Don't feel too bad about this donation."

"Don't I even get half?"

"Hell, *I'm* not a philanthropist."

13

The closest thing to a city that he had seen in some time, Saint Auban had several cinemas, book stores, and even a real estate office. Men and women walked around in decent clothes, and only by their thinness was it possible to know that they had suffered in the war. MPs weren't everywhere, which was a blessing.

"I want to get a good meal at a table," Jeff said.

"Not me."

"What do you want?"

"Some nice ass."

"Are you on that tack again? Not that I mind, if the girl is all right; but I want to be comfortable, too."

"Plenty of time for that when you're dead."

The street was jammed with traffic. Cars, bicycles, battered taxis, trucks, all moved slowly. Jeff, with his previous experience, looked around for the sight of hungry children without seeing any who didn't look decently fed, if hollow-eyed.

"Pretty far behind the lines," Ryder said. "They were okay down here, and they could survive the war and the occupation if they weren't Jewish. Not easy, but it could be done."

It was a cloudy day, and the tree-lined streets were dim. Having registered at an army billet without any trouble, Ryder wanted to go on the town immediately.

Jeff held out for a sit-down dinner, and enjoyed it enormously at a small restaurant with creaky chairs and scarred tables. The food wasn't much, but Jeff didn't complain. Ryder, who hadn't eaten in comfort since God knew when, complained all the time.

"We're wasting time," Ryder insisted.

"As soon as I finish this chicory, or whatever it is, we'll go out."

"Well, hurry the hell up."

The tree-lined streets looked dim on this cloudy day. Ryder, who had talked to a GI while they were registering, was looking at buildings they passed.

"Here's the place," he said. "Hold on, and I'll see if I can fix us up."

A group of teenage boys were standing on a corner and talking languidly. At Jeff's smiling approach, the nearest one frowned and turned away disapprovingly before walking off.

One of them had left a swatch of cloth on the ground. Jeff picked it up and glanced along the street, hoping that the boy would come back for it. An older man began shouting at him and a crowd formed as quickly as would have happend back home in Queens. Men and women scowled at Jeff and muttered. There wasn't a GI in the crowd, so Jeff resigned himself to hearing a middle-aged man shout at him in a foreign language.

The man suddenly shoved him against part of the crowd and the people he landed against shoved him back. Jeff put thumb and second finger of the left hand into his mouth for a shrill whistle in hope that some Yank or local *gendarme* might show up.

As soon as the French saw him getting ready to signal, they drew back. The crowd was becoming thinner. There was a man in French Army uniform at the perimeter, and Jeff wondered if he had persuaded the others to go about their business with some swift and angry words.

The Frenchman, a colonel, was only a few years older than Jeff. Gravely he accepted a salute and returned it in good form. He wore a row of battle decorations.

"You did not make yourself popular," he said in accented English.

"Some kids were standing around and when one of them left this thing here, I picked it up and figured I'd give it back to the kid when he came back for it. The crowd came instead."

"Ah, I see." The colonel's smile showed gold teeth. "Americans are popular, but the people are so used to having been cheated and used barbarously—as over there."

There was a three-sided yard across the street, the sides covered with sandbags.

"That is where the Germans dealt with enemies of their state -- Jews, gypsies, and so on." The colonel pointed to the revolvers on his hips and gestured a trigger being squeezed. "I see another American coming in our direction, so I feel I can leave you now. Good luck, private."

"Thank you, and the same to you—to all of you."

"The French are not free because they were lucky, nor were they enslaved for the same reason. But I appreciate your sentiment."

Jeff was still staring at the execution area when Ryder swaggered over to him.

"Come on, Part, you look like you've been frozen," his buddy said. "I'm pretty sure we can get us some women in a little while. First of all, we need more francs. Come on."

Jeff didn't say a word until they had left that particular neighborhood. Ryder was looking arund as if he expected to see old friends on the long street.

"Who are you looking for?"

"A street peddler to change currency for us."

"But I'm sure they'll cheat," Jeff protested. "If I've heard O'Caffie's song and dance on the subject once, you must've been through it a million times."

"Two million—but who counts? Believe in Uncle Gil, Part, and you'll see how even the crookedest street peddler can be honest."

His sharp eyes spotted a furtive-looking man who needed a shave. The man glanced from left to right as he approached at Ryder's signal. Ryder had put himself several steps ahead of Jeff.

"You need local money," he said carefully. "The occupation forces give bad rates. Pierre Mansour, he give good rates to the Yanks, who deliver us."

"Do you give four francs to the dollar?"

"For the Americans, five francs to the dollar."

"Jeff, we've found an honest man, even a generous man. I told you we would."

"But this matter must not be observed." the peddler said, leading the way to the threshold of a closed flower shop with two semi-circular display windows. Ryder passed across a five dollar bill. Pierre Mansour held it up to the light, nodded, then drew out a fistful of franc notes from a ragged looking pocket. As he counted, Jeff, who had joined them, saw that the peddler was doubling up bills in order to pass off one as two. Gaining in self-confidence, he tripled up on the bills. At this rate they'd be lucky to get half their money's worth. Ryder didn't seem to notice Jeff's frantic signals.

"Hey, pal," Ryder said slowly, "When you get done, I'm going to count those notes very careful, and my buddy will stand here to keep you from leaving our company too quick."

"*Je ne comprends pas*," the peddler said too quickly. "I no understand."

"If there should be less than twenty-five franc notes in the bundle, me and my friend are going to turn you over to the gendarmes."

The currency peddler sighed, then shrugged.

"You think you can talk your way out of a jail term because you'll have only cheated Americans, and though they liberated you they aren't members of that big and exlcusive club of Frenchmen." The peddler's grin was swiftly hidden, and Ryder smiled. "But before we turn you over, you'll be black and blue. Me and my buddy will see to that."

"To do violence is illegal."

"*Je ne comprends pas*," Ryder said blandly in a miserable accent. "I think we understand each other, pal. And don't forget we're out of sight and can cover you and work real fast. You insisted on privacy."

The peddler sighed more deeply this time and started the count again. Ryder earned a few times the going rate.

"Do you want some of this action too, Part? You won't beat Pierre's personal rate of exchange."

"I'll take another flier."

The peddler looked horrified. "Gentlemen, I beg your pardon, but only an honest businessman should attempt to deal with you, and I regret not to qualify. If I do much more business of this kind, I expect to be ruined."

Jeff and Ryder laughed. Jeff couldn't resist drawing out a dollar bill and saying, "Here's a tip for you." He stood aside to let the peddler run off and scuttle up the street, followed by the sound of their laughter.

"What we want to buy is a commodity—right?" Ryder asked briskly. "Then the best place to go is to the top market in Saint Auban."

Jeff, who was imagining a slave market for tattooed women who were veterans of concentration camps, hesitated.

"I got the whole story back in that building where I went to," Ryder said confidently. "You'll have a broad next to you before the night is over."

Jeff wondered if he would ever like a French town, and supposed that when he was old he would remember the places with affection. All he saw on the short walk were buildings that had been gutted, sandbags, MPs, frantic little children whose faces showed no joy, women with pinched eyes, and few men. Most of those were over-age, but the younger ones seemed cheerful and sleek and some of them even well-fed.

Ryder must have been following Jeff's emotions as they scampered across this features. "There are good people and bad out here, just like anyplace else. The French take care of number one, but they're patriotic. I wouldn't say it's abandoning the human race to keep an eye out for number one."

The town that had seemed so normal and relaxed at first sight had turned into another example of war behind the lines. Little merchandise could be seen in the shops, women offered themselves but found few takers, and the churches seemed to have no windows. It was the number of churches that surprised Jeff more than anything else he saw; there seemed to be a church and a bakery on every block.

"Here's the dump we want, Part."

It was a dim-lit bar. Girls sat around, drinking tea out of whiskey glasses, waiting for a customer to join them in a drink. A set of stairs began at the bar's exact centre, making for an implication that not even Jeff could possibly misunderstand. The girls wore dresses and nothing under them. It seemed to Jeff that their hearts were beating, but their eyes were dead.

"Which one do you like best, Part?" Ryder asked, waving a hand expansively. "Pick any one."

A girl sitting halfway between stairs and bar had a fragile look and wore a flower in her hair. Not the prettiest girl in the room, but Jeff thought she looked neater and cleaner than the rest.

Ryder walked over as soon as Jeff picked her out. He talked for a minute, gesturing at the notes in his pocket. Jeff, who had expected that Ryder would want to trade food or stockings for any girl's favors, was surprised that it was so simple. The girl glanced from him to Jeff and back again, then nodded and stood up and walked toward the stairs. She hadn't cracked a smile.

As he followed Ryder he asked, "Is this all?"

"It's the introduction, kid. There's better to follow."

There was a hallway, and the girl gestured for Ryder to stop, then murmured a few words.

"She's going to make sure the room is clear," he told Jeff as the girl started down the corridor.

"I would think they'd know right away by

signals," Jeff said. "I's bad business to keep a customer waiting in this kind of place."

"Part, you could be right. I think we'd better be damn caref—what the fuck!"

The lights went out just as Ryder started over to the stairtop again. Jeff had already wheeled around in that direction. He felt a weight close to him and hit out. Ryder was doing the same. The room was so dark that he was worried he might hit Ryder instead of an attacker, but there didn't seem any need to worry. Again and again he struck out and heard profanity in a foreign voice.

Ryder must have been the one who suddenly turned and kicked out and opened a door, throwing so much light onto the hallway that it was possible to move clearly. Two men lay on the floor, breathing hard. A third sat on the floor, one hand gripping his stomach, the other flailing at the air. As Jeff watched briefly, that man threw up, the vomit dribbling down his jacket and pants to the dirty floor.

"Trying to clean us," Ryder said, disgusted. "Well, if they ever come out to my neck of the woods I can show *them* a few pretty good con games, too."

"They'll probably make enough money to retire and go to the French Riviera."

"They'll be falling for the biggest con game there ever was, this side of the stock market. Serve 'em right, too, and to hell with 'em. Do me a little favor, Part, will you?"

"Sure."

"When you walk down the stairs and start out, do like I will and try to look as if you didn't get cheated, but you got laid."

"Sure," Jeff said, and didn't laugh.

They discovered the ad in the first place because Ryder took it into his head to buy a glass monkey no bigger than a baby's thumb. He pulled out two francs to pay for the thing in a small store, and suddenly found the notes snatched out of his hand. A starved-looking boy with hollow cheeks was trying to run. Jeff could have caught him, but let the boy go. He had been carrying newspapers in a hand, apparently to sell, and dropped half a dozen of them.

Jef picked one up. "At least you got something for your money."

Ryder surprised him by taking it. In the street he riffled through the few thin pages, looking knowledgeably at the news items.

"God bless the Americans and British and the Free French, and business as usual." Ryder had come to the last page, where his interest sharpened. "Ads. Personals."

"Is that good or bad?"

"A broad or two is sure to advertise, and there might be some hope in that."

"Sure. *All* our money will be stolen." He remembered a gag line that Oliver Hardy was always using to Stan Laurel. "Here's another fine mess you got us into."

Ryder wasn't listening. He was able to make out the words—if very slowly—in the news ads.

" 'Young lady, twenty-six, seeks gentleman with dowry.' Forget that!"

"I'd like to dowry *her*," Jeff said, with unusual vehemence. "Besides, I thought that only a woman came with a dowry."

"I did, too. Maybe I'm reading it wrong. 'Woman, 32, seeks position as nurse.' No, ma'am, not with me."

"She ought to join the Free French."

" 'Young woman, 24, attractive, seeks husband.' Then there's something I can't make out, and an address."

"I'm surprised you aren't on the way over there, already."

"This much I'll tell you, Part. The word husband might mean that a boy friend will do, and the age is right. She wants something, all right, and Uncle Gil has no objections to letting her have it."

"Are you really going to see her?"

"I'll give her a chance to see me."

"Good luck."

"Come on, kid, and let's see what happens. If she's good to look at, you can find out how to approach a broad. And who's to say she wouldn't have a friend for you? Let me get that address right."

They found the girl working as a reception clerk in a hotel with few patrons on a side street. It didn't take much guessing to realize what the hotel was mainly used for.

The girl's name was Nichette and to call her a beauty would have been one of the year's understatements. She was a knockout, with skin smooth as pearl and eyes whose inner light washed across Jeff like a beacon.

When Ryder told her that he had come over in response to her newspaper add, Nichette turned away long enough to arrange for another clerk to take over behind the desk. She led Ryder into a small room with two chairs, not making any comment about Jeff's presence. Jeff wouldn't have come inside with them, but Ryder was vain enough to insist on it.

"The ad said you wanted a husband." Ryder accented the last word in his atrocious French.

"That is correct," Her English was surprisingly attractive, and the tones seemed to send vibrations up and down Jeff's spine.

"Well, I figure that you and the guy will have to try each other out for a while. I'm willing to give you a try and see that you've got whatever you need during that time. And if you could find a friend of yours for Private Parton over here, we'd all be tickled."

"I am flattered." Nichette appeared to be considering what she'd heard. "Are you an engineer?"

"When it comes to dealing with broa—women, I'm pretty much of an engineer."

"No, we speak against each other." Nichette slapped her thighs with strong but attractive hands. "I am twenty-four years of age and quite good looking. I have realized that it is time for me to improve myself, and so I advertised for a husband with the provision that he must be an engineer. I know that such a man will provide well for me, and I have much to offer in return."

Ryder's face fell. "A few words in that ad of yours I couldn't make out at all, and I suppose them were the words."

"Quite so." She glanced at his right sleeve. "I would be willing to go to the United States, but not with a private first class who wouldn't qualify."

"Sorry."

"Hard decisions must be followed through."

"Do you have any friends?"

"Alas, no! Would a girl of ordinary looks befriend a beauty?"

Jeff was out of that room and back in the once-luxurious lobby by the time a grim-lipped Ryder strode out.

"With a beautiful piece like that, I should've known there'd be some gimmick," he said. "Why didn't you take a crack at her? You're more the Joe College type than I'll ever be."

"I don't know why I didn't," Jeff muttered.

"Scared, huh? Didn't you tell me once that you were going to college before the army threw a lasso on you?"

"At nights. I wanted to be an accountant, not an engineer.

"Well, you could have lied a little." Ryder pursed his lips. "Tell you what, Part. Would you be interested in that French cupcake?"

"Who wouldn't?"

"Well, if you want her, I'll see you get her. Hell, I'm scrubbed out over there. I might just as well help a buddy along. What are buddies for, after all?"

Are you serious?"

"Uh-huh. There's a hotel two blocks down, the Lille; I noticed it on the way over. It's on the Rue du Marechal. Register and get a room. Then wait."

"What are you going to do?"

"I'll tell her that I was testing her for your sake and that you're a shy student of engineering. I'll tell her she has to go see you and bring her over if I can. You ought to be okay for tonight, anyhow. At least one of us will be."

"Shoud I register under my own name?"

"Of course not. You don't want to give any of these broads a chance to find out who you really are. Call yourself Jeffrey Quick. That'll be about right. After all, the whole thing is going to be a quickie. Now get to the hotel and register and wait. I'm going back right now to talk to the broad."

The hotel wasn't bad looking, even if it wasn't up to the standards of the Astor back in New York City. The rooms were neat and reasonably airy, and Jeff spent time making sure that his room would be spotless. He was especially careful about the bed, cleaning under it with more conscientiousness than any housemaid.

Time passed, and he finally ordered dinner in his room. Nichette didn't put in an appearance, and he was getting groggy. At half-past eleven he sank like lead into the one soft chair and promptly fell asleep.

A series of short knocks on the door awakened him. Daylight was coming through the slitted blinds. He spared a glance for the only soft bed he had seen in at least a month. Gil Ryder was on the other side of the door, smiling warmly as he stepped in.

"Sorry about this," he said. "Them's the breaks of the game, though."

"What do you mean?"

"You're going to hate me for dotting the i's and crossing the t's, Part, so you'd better lend me some money before we go any further place.

"Ten bucks enough?"

"Fine . . . . Well, you can probably come damn close to guessing what happened. Me and Nichette got to talking and what with one thing and another we shacked up. She's pretty damn good, that girl."

Jeff looked bitterly at the chair on which he had stretched out for the night. "You're a pal."

"It just happened, Part. I wasn't trying to bug you or anybody else. Me and Nichette had hot pants for each other, and that's all there is to it."

"But she said that all she wanted was to marry an engineer."

"I told her I'm an engineer in human relations, and there's no professional need for me in the Army. Hell, if a carny talker isn't a human relations engineer, then nobody is. What in hell is so funny?"

"Nothing, Ryder. Nothing at all."

"So I'll see you on the way back, " Ryder said slowly. "I've got me six days to howl, and I'm going to howl for every damned one of em. You should make out better on your own than with me."

"Okay." Jeff hesitated. "Do you need more money?"

"Do you mean that you'd lend me more after what I. . .? Part, you're a real pal. How much genuine moolah have you got with you?"

"Sixty-three bucks, give or take a few nickels and dimes."

"Well, I don't want to be unfair," Ryder said thoughtfully. "Let's split it."

After Ryder left, Jeff took his clothes off and fell across the bed and shut his eyes. The bed turned out to be too damned soft. He couldn't sleep.

14

After a shower Jeff checked out of the hotel and headed for the U.S. Army billet. Somebody from the outfit was sure to be there and he wouldn't have to spend six days alone in a city where everybody spoke French. He'd rather sit with a glowering Anse Tarves or hear Mort Kaplan describe brand-new symptoms.

Two blocks from the billet somebody shouted at him, "Hey, Jeff!"

"Sam! Where in hell have you been?"

He had known Sam Avakian since basic training and the two of them had watched each other climb poles with full packs on or crawl under barbed wire with bayonets at the ready while bullets whistled over their heads.

"I'm in Hotel Company, the Sixteenth," Sam said.

"Baker for me."

"That makes us *landsmen*." Sam's face turned serious. "Listen, Jeff, I got screwed by some of these currency hotshots out here, and I'm good as broke."

"You can have ten bucks American any time." Jeff handed it over, feeling a little disappointed that somebody as smart as Sam had let himself get fooled. "You can have a drink, too."

"As long as it isn't any of that lousy wine. I tell you I'm starting to piss beaujolais I've had so much of it."

Jeff realized he was doing the leading, as Ryder did with him. In a bar, where overhead fans revolved slowly, they talked about platoon members they recalled. Some of them were out here, a few others were fighting the Japs, one had been killed in a training accident, two were prisoners of the krauts. Jeff, listening, thanked his lucky stars he'd had the friendship and good advice of an experienced soldier to fall back on.

Since Sam didn't know what he wanted to do that day, Jeff suggested that they might start by going to church. Avakian, who was a Catholic, cheerfully agreed and made some bad jokes about Jeff's likely reception.

There was an argument with the bartender, Avakian talking thirteen to the dozen—it seemed that every U.S. soldier was handy with the language except Jeff. Half a dozen people gathered around, including some from the outside.

Jeff murmured, "Is everybody in this goddam country after us?"

A girl came forward out of the crowd. She wore a long-sleeved, high-necked dress slit to the hips. Her skin was light, her eyes almond-shaped, and her hair seemed to have the texture of lace.

"Gentlemen," the vision said in English, with only a trace of accent, "you have disturbed some of our good citizens. I feel sure it was not intentional."

"Bet your ass it wasn't," Avakian started, "but this here highbinder—"

The matter was settled very quickly, with the girl's help. Avakian paid over a few more coins and received an added drink. The crowd dispersed, and Jeff spoke to the girl as she was starting to leave.

"Aren't I ever going to see you again?"

"It is probably better that you shouldn't."

"How can you be sure?"

The girl walked off, but turned to see him stare

after her. She smiled and walked away again.

Jeff was overdue for some good luck, and it came his way when he least expected it. He was leading Sam Avakian to the end of the block when he saw the same girl on her way back. She looked calm, but her lips were tight with anger.

He waited for her to reach him and then asked, "Is anything wrong?"

"One cannot walk in that direction," she said quietly. "The Germans left behind a delayed action bomb, which was found on time. But the police are looking for others."

"Maybe I can take you someplace," he offered. "Only too glad to help."

"Perhaps you can."

As they walked off, Jeff paused to wave so long to a suddenly crushed Sam Avakian. It took a while before he realized that they were headed toward the building that served as the army billet.

"Do you work for the Army?"

"In a clerical capacity." She smiled. "My parents wouldn't permit that I learn the more strenuous types of work."

"And your name?"

"I am called Fanchon Ribadeau."

Jeff gave his name, and with more nerve than he'd ever felt in the presence of a girl, added, "You're going to have dinner with me and show me this city."

"Am I?" she murmured.

"Yes, or I'll get you fired. I'm one of your bosses, don't forget."

She laughed gracefully.

The rest of that afternoon consisted of Jeff walking around while waiting for Fanchon to be finished with work. He went to a Catholic church, and saw a silent film with an actress named Marion Davies. It was seven o'clock when the last guard cleared Fanchon to leave the billet. She looked as fresh as when Jeff had first seen her.

Dinner was eaten at an inexpensive restaurant, and wasn't much except for the ubiquitous wine. There was no dancing and nothing like a concert, an opera, or a stage performance. He took Fanchon to see a French film and suffered through it, not having the slightest idea what was happening.

He took Fanchon home, but was not permitted inside the small house where she lived with her parents. He didn't kiss her or even touch her. Fanchon agreed to guide him for the next few days when she wasn't working or sleeping. They agreed to meet in front of a flower shop on the Rue du Monsieur.

For Jeff it was the beginning of the first happy adventure he had known since going to summer camp as a child. Through Fanchon's eyes he saw and understood the many things which were different among these people he had been on the point of despising. A hard life for the men and an even harder one for most of the women had been the result of the soul-destroying conflict that had sown death and destruction everywhere. The only synagogue in the city had been taken over by the Nazis, who had felt great delight in using it for a bawdy house.

It had been a difficult life, before the Germans came—a life with few expectations, but at least there was mutual respect among the French people.

"Did the Germans change all that?"

"They did." It had become difficult to keep any footing. People were liable to be informed upon by those who envied a house or coveted a daughter. Men and women, sometimes whole families, simply disappeared. In those circumstances, people looked at their lifetime friends and neighbors with fear and hatred. The crime rate had gone up considerably, with men killing because they felt someone might inform on them. Oddly enough, the petty crime rates had gone down.

"What about the F.F.I.?" Jeff asked, "The resistance. The *maquis*."

The French resistance had never really gained a foothold in Saint Auban, and it was hard to say why. Perhaps families felt so isolated from the rest of France, the rest of the world. Perhaps they felt that they would live through this plague, too. And in the back of their minds was a belief that only criminals would be harmed; and this in spite of the examples of the gypsies and the Jews of their town. People didn't learn—perhaps they didn't care in the last analysis. Perhaps it was like what was said about war, that no one truly believed *he* would be killed.

Jeff brought the conversation around to another subject altogether . . . .

The evening he went into a French home was a distinct triumph for him—at least in the beginning. It was the home of Fanchon's parents, of course, and nothing that he saw matched what he had expected. Madame Ribadeau was of an oriental cast. There was a three-tiered altar draped by a red, yellow, blue, and white Buddhist flag. On the lowest rung were pictures of older people and brass candlesticks shaped like storks, in holders that looked like turtles. Incense was being burned in the center rung. The highest tier carried what Jeff supposed was a painted representation of the Buddha.

"One should be reminded of traditions," Monsieur Ribadeau said easily, noticing Jeff's muffled astonishment.

"Are you a Buddhist?"

"I have become a believer, with my wife, in Cao Dai." The small and dapper and well-mannered Monsieur Ribadeau smiled easily.

"Then what makes you keep Buddhist relics in your home?"

"Let me explain something of the nature of Cao Dai," Monsieur Ribadeau said over the modest dinner. "Cao Dai itself is a form of understanding and harmonizing the world's religions. We believe that there is much in the way of goodness and decency and charity to be learned from all of them, that all religions contain part of the True Way, but that no one is the complete answer by itself."

"But I suppose that you worship Buddha."

"Cao Dai has reverence for Buddhism because there is much to be learned from it. But it also has reverence for Jesus Christ, for Moses, and -- you may scoff at this -- a high place in the Cao Dai pantheon is reserved for the writer, Victor Hugo."

"I don't see a cross in your home. And I suppose it wouldn't be smart to have a star of David."

"I was born a Christian, my wife was born a Buddhist, but I have chosen the way of all our ancestors to remind us of them." Fanchon's father hesitated. "Perhaps you will fully understand when you grow older. Perhaps much of this unhappy country is too difficult to understand."

Monsieur Ribadeau switched the conversation to secular subjects. It turned out that the mild-mannered little man was a police official, and Jeff said that real life crime wasn't like detective stories. Ribadeau astonished him by shaking his head.

"On the whole, no, but every so often a truly fantastic case transpires."

"For instance?"

"I remember one that is only six months old. There was this man—we will call him Smith. That is your English version of Jacques Bonhomme, everyman, is it not?"

"Smith. Jones. Robinson."

"So! M. Smith is in his fifties, and a chemist, so he is able to survive the occupation as far as the Germans are concerned. During the first week of February, the office manager in the laboratory where he worked asked his secretary if M. Smith had left him the day's notes to be typed up by one of the girls. The secretary said that the notes had not been left. The office manager told her that before going home for the day she should go to M. Smith's office and check him out. M. Smith was fond on the ladies and they of him, so she hurried over there. She found him."

Jeff, who would rather have looked at Fanchon, found his interest caught.

"Was he dead?"

"He was not sleeping. Three times he had been shot in the stomach. He didn't have any strength left after the third shot, hardly enough to speak of, so he crawled over to the laboratory table and picked up a dark pencil—the doctors confirm this—and on the surface of the desk he wrote down who had killed him."

"Like in a movie, you mean?" Now Jeff's interest was definitely caught. "That's fantastic!"

"Quite so. What he wrote down was the letter M, with a period after it, and then started to draw a half-circle that was obviously the conclusion of the name. For instance, it might have been an O or C—impossible to tell."

"What did you do?"

"First we examined the room. It had a table, a high

chair, notes with symbols and almost cruelly clear lighting. The killer had knocked on the door, which Smith generally kept locked. Smith went to it, opened it, and the killer shot him and left by the back of the establishment."

"How do you know that?"

"The outside door was left open and one of my men found a PPK-Walther with a silencer, all on the sidewalk where somebody had pitched it down. Smith was killed by that gun. More to the point, a witness saw the murderer leaving."

"How would he know that? The witness, I mean."

"Well, he didn't know it was a murderer he saw until later on. It seems there'd been emergency excavation work going on in part of the gutter on the street that the back way leads out to—a result of Allied bombing, indeed. One of the men looked up and saw a man in a coat and hat with a pulled-down brim. That man was running out the back way of the building. The witness saw this man drop something into the sewer grating and then run to the corner out of sight."

"Did you check up on the witness himself?"

"He was just a member of a labor gang whom the Boche had recruited. He knew nothing. Indeed, he had originally come from the city of Brest, I believe, and been uprooted by the war."

"Like everybody else." Jeff shrugged. "And then what did you do?"

"Ah, it was necessary to notify the widow of the good Mr. Smith. As the *sous-commissaire* of the police forces, I took this job upon myself. One never knows what a woman will tell that is helpful if she is too upset to control herself. Mrs. Smith was a good-looking woman in her thirties. She took the news bravely, and suggested that I talk to the family lawyer to find out about M. Smith's will. The woman's voice became warmer when she mentioned the lawyer."

"You must have been suspicious."

"Indeed I was. Michel Lechat had been interested in Mme. Smith for a while, but she was satisfied with her husband. There are men who frolic as they wish, and keep their wives happy as well. A matter of good fortune."

"Did you arrest Lechat?"

"I questioned him severely, but learned nothing that would be of help in a prosecution. True, an accused person is considered guilty until proven otherwise, but there is no case to be made out this time, none whatever."

"Did you check out Smith's past to see if he had made enemies?"

"Indeed, yes. No clues resulted."

"Did you question anyone else?"

"Well, we searched for a culprit, a Monsieur someone whom the dead man had started to name and who was seen at the time the murder took place and who disposed of the fatal gun. We questioned the office manager, one Maurice—ah, let us call him Jones, in line with our conceit at the start. The office manager had sent home the secretary who found the body after she became sick. As a result, M. Jones was short-handed."

"Did you question him vigorously?"

"Very much so. He told me about Smith's extramarital affairs, and that Smith had lived some years of hie life in America, which had made the Germans wary of employing him. Very much so, I understand."

"Did he spend his early life in America, this Smith of yours?"

"His first ten years." Ribadeau sighed. "I wish he had been a better witness to his own murder."

Jeff said, "He might have been a good enough witness as it is."

"And I misunderstood? But how is that possible?"

"If he lived his early years in America then at the last minutes he may have reverted to American ways and—"

"Ah, I see, I see!" Ribadeau snapped his fingers. "Indeed, yes. Permit me to construct the crime anew, as it must have taken place."

"Of course."

"Smith was a buccaneer with women, so he looked around the place in which he worked in order to see what adventures he might find. The woman who is secretary to M. Jones is young and attractive."

"Could the girl have killed him?"

"Yes, I think so. She excused herself from work for a little while, put on flat shoes if she wasn't already wearing them, wiped make-up from her face and went to the lockers for a man's coat and hat. She put them on, went to the door of the laboratory, knocked. Smith answered. He was shot. The secretary—we call her Miss Ribson—ran outside, leaving the door opened to show that the killer escaped by the back way. She is sure that one of the labor gang outside will see a man running. She drops the gun into the sewer, runs to the corner, turns and slows down, then goes back into the place by the front entrance. She puts back the man's coat and hat in the locker and puts on high-heeled shoes and make-up again. She is ready. Probably she wasn't used to all that exercise, and the strain of the run and the killing made her sick. She had to leave the office after the body was found."

"And the man who'd been shot—Smith? What about him?"

"Here you speak to the point, my young American

friend. He writes the last message, memory reverting to his United States upbringing. He writes the letter of the first name of his killer—the secretary's first name happens to be Madeleine. Before he can write her second name, he dies."

"Can you prove it at all?"

"With the idea of yours, it should be simple. I find out if Smith had an affair with Miss Robinson, and if he had backed away afterwards. I tell her that I have proof she left fingerprints on the hat and coat she used, and I think she admits the truth of my construction of the case. A very sensitive woman, you know, high-strung."

As Monsieur Ribadeau sat back in a satisfied way, Jeff reminded him who had been of such help.

"I'm glad I was able to make a difference."

"Your aid has been material," Monsieur Ribadeau beamed, and he turned to Fanchon. "My child, this young man has my full approval as a beau for you."

As Ryder would have said, the point had been made the hard way.

Jeff was beginning to feel a pleasant glow when he considered Fanchon Ribadeau. He had even looked up the rules for marrying while in the Army. It seemed that he'd have to get his Captain's permission and then the girl would take a medical examination and security check. There would be a three-to-four month waiting period. Forty-five days after the marriage took place, the girl would be able to come to America.

Unless he'd misread the whole business.

He got out of bed on that morning, wishing that she was close to him, then shook himself. He might want the girl, might even be a little in love—but he'd be damned if he'd marry her.

All the same he was due to see her and say so long. It was the last day of his leave, and the two had agreed on a light lunch together at a restaurant called Dupont's, on the Rue d'Afrique.

The block before the restaurant was cordoned off. An Australian in a British uniform told Jeff that a delayed action bomb left by the Germans had gone off, killing four women, seven children, and the soldier's best friend.

Jeff couldn't get through the barrier. If Fanchon had come here, she had taken one look at the obstruction and left. It occurred to him that a bomb attempt several days before had brought the two of them together, and now a bombing would keep them apart. Maybe that was the right way for their friendship to finish.

But he looked back at the barricades for a long time as he walked off.

Arriving at the billet a few minutes after Ryder, he saw that the older man looked tired. His hatchet face was unshaven. He shook hands listlessly.

"Sorry about everything, Part," he said.

"No real harm done."

"You got yourself another broad, Part, huh? I told you there's plenty of ass all over this burg."

"I guess so."

"Mine was great. You remember her, Part, don't you? The one with that ad in the paper?"

"Sure I remember."

"She was *fantastic*. I thought I knew something about sex, but she showed me things I never even guessed. She's a great kid, Nichette is, if you don't get weak."

"Are you seeing her again?"

"I'll find another broad. Why get mixed up with only one? Especially when you need a fortune to play her."

"You didn't have a whole hell of a lot of money with you this time, Ryder."

"Damn right. And when it ran out, so did—well, never mind. Tell me about your piece of quail, Part. Good looking?"

Jeff gave the answers mechanically and in such a way as to exclude any real information. As a green painted truck took them back to hell, Jeff realized that, without any sexual involvement, he'd managed to have a better time than Ryder. He wished he'd been able to get Fanchon into the sack, but what the hell!

What the hell!

15

"Things have been too damn quiet," Captain West said irritably. "The krauts have gone back into a bottle of horseradish and pulled the cap on over them."

The other men at the CP listened with the respect owed to a captain. West had called in Lieutenant Hearn, the company commanders, and the first sergeants for one of his night briefings.

"We all know what's happened," he said, walking up and down. "We've put so much pressure on the kraut in the last months that he's hitting back sporadically instead of giving direct battle where we can hurt by killing."

"How do we get him into direct action, sir?" Lieutenant Hearn asked.

"I've given some thought to that, and I see only one answer. We have to set up a situation where he wants to destroy. We all know what they'd hate the most—or do we?"

"Jews, you mean? Gypsies, maybe?"

"Damn few Jews or gypsies left, Hearn, and they wouldn't prove anything if we could track 'em down. No, what we need is to start rebuilding."

"That's true. Old Adolf himself foams at the mouth if he thinks we're trying to help some people around here, and actually doing a job."

"Then what we have to do is find a small town or a village that's located favorably for our purpose and help put it together again. That'll bring jerry out and roaring, if I'm any judge."

Hearn asked slowly, "So we set these people up as a decoy in hopes that the kraut will smash everything. Is that it?"

"Try to smash everything, Hearn. He's not to be allowed to get away with it."

"That kind of help doesn't amount to much, then."

"In a war situation, Hearn, nothing amounts to much except killing the enemy." Captain West hesitated. "Tomorrow morning I want a jeep taken out and some recon work done. We've got to be damn careful in picking the right village."

The rebuilding program in the village of Louque started two days after Captain West's personal recon job. Louque was some twenty-five miles from the next village, so small it prompted one of the men to remark that dirt was its leading product. The job was going to be long and tedious, and very few of the fighting men knew its real purpose.

The men of Hotel Company organized a scrub-in for the kids, setting up a place in the center of the village. The youngsters were scared at first sight of so much soap, which made them feel as if they were being tickled, but they were soon chortling with delight and showing off their cleanliness to the grown-ups. Great quantities of GI soap changed hands before the day was out.

After the medics held one examination of all the people, Dr. Fortune was flown in to look at the more severe cases.

The men went to work with a will, repairing a bomb-shattered bridge and digging a well. It wasn't easy to make sense out of the sanitation facilities the way the Nazis had left them.

The whole job took time. September passed into October. The villagers, suspicious at first, had become grateful and friendly. New homes had been built. Plans were being laid to set off part of the south village for an orphanage to be staffed by nuns who had lost their Order in the dregs of war.

The main opposition to the program seemed to be coming from the Army itself. It started because of Dr. Fortune's zeal to do his job. The small, fierce, dedicated doctor who had stuck his neck out against the official enemy numberless times, was willing to take on his own army if it insisted on making trouble.

In one of his medical examinations he found that a twenty-two year old woman needed emergency surgery. Fortune arranged to have her flown behind the lines to the nearest American hospital.

Captain West saw her being put into the plane and asked Fortune, "Why aren't you working inside the village like you're supposed to?"

"The woman needs surgery right away or she won't live."

"You're supposed to work inside the village. You're one of the officers who knows it."

"Captain, you're not telling the engineers how to get their jobs done, so leave the medical personnel alone too. You want a job done, and that's what you're getting."

"I don't want our hospital filled up with foreign

civilians."

"One person only takes up one bed," Fortune said brusquely. "That's simple arithmetic."

The surgery was successful, and a few days later it was followed by surgery to repair a young woman's cleft palate. If there was any grumbling by the men in hospital, Fortune made a point of not hearing it.

He started taking other local patients to the hospital. He and the orthopedist did a series of tendon repairs on a small boy. Fortune himself took out a mortar fragment from an area deep in the brain of another child. The surgical staff worked on those cases between handling battle casualties among the GIs, and they worked carefully.

When part of the hospital was cordoned off for the bedding of women patients, enemies of the plan said that it wasn't helpful for the GIs to know that so many women were close by, and incidents were sure to take place. When Fortune took children's cases only, the critics' argument was that children were too noisy for the best treatment of GI casualties. West, his patience finally worn thin, demanded that no more child cases be accepted.

Fortune instantly obtained the help of the engineers in planning a children's hospital near the base. It was finally decided to let him take over a QM building for the purpose.

West came to see the doctor as soon as word got through to him. "I don't want you or the rest of the base staff taking time from the treatment of our men, doctor. Dammit, one reason I'm here is to see the Army gets the maximum service out of everybody in it."

"Does it occur to you," Fortune asked quietly, "that doing such work is the best possible therapy for the doctors themselves? If they see nothing but casualties, they're bound to get battle fatigue."

"How do you think the men feel, knowing that their doctors aren't giving them all their attention?"

Fortune considered that. "It would be a damn shame if they're upset, but every patient in this hospital needs help."

"Our men need the fullest attention."

"In my opinion, they're getting everything that's possible."

West said stiffly, "I'll apply for guidance from Washington. In the meantime I want you to delay all plans for a children's hospital and not admit any more civilian patients. I hate to put it in these terms, but that's an order; and if you won't obey it I can have your ass put in a sling."

Fortune admitted five other cases in the next few days, including another candidate for cleft palate surgery. He and the engineers ran themselves ragged trying to get together enough spare beds for the children's hospital.

He was conferring with an X-ray technician about a flak wound on an A-23 pilot when Captain West appeared, a paper in his hand. Fortune was genuinely startled to see the Captain looking triumphant.

"This will confirm," West said coldly, "that you are to deal with no patients whatever except on an emergency basis—that is, no civilian patients. No more cleft palate cases or hangnails or whatever you've been taking in. There is to be no expansion of hospital facilities at the base in the near future. I am empowered to take what action I see fit if this order is disobeyed."

Dr. Fortune finished his conference with the X-ray man, then turned to the order and read every word of it. His small face was deathly white when he looked up.

"Congratulations, captain," he said bitterly. "You and a half a dozen other shmucks have won a colossal victory."

16

The Germans waited until mid-October before using mortars against the town, killing two men and wounding five. A patrol operation was mounted by Hotel Company, and while the enemy was avoiding them the job was easy. The job got harder when a German company abruptly opened fire and killed every man in the lead squad.

The men of Hotel Company ducked for cover, most of them finding it in back of trees that smelled like pancake batter dipped in the eternal wine. The Germans mounted the first of what was to be a series of human-wave attacks, but Hotel Company stood its ground and gave them the sort of withering gunfire that almost made up for the damage that had already been done.

So many bullets were used in a short time that Captain West got the impression there was a danger of shortage. West had the radioman call for an airlift of munitions and the job was done despite the risk of heavy gunfire.

Under cover of a called-in air strike, reinforcements from Baker Company landed at a point behind the Germans positions and opened up with BAR fire. Artillery had been synchronized, and now it was brought into action.

The Battle of Perrier, as it has been called after the

nearest town, gave rise to stories and incidents that the survivors have remembered for the rest of their lives. PFC Andrew Spicehandler was caught short of ammo and had to strangle two jerries with his bare hands. Private Sam Melton, caught short too, picked up what looked like a large fork and knocked half a dozen Germans unconscious. When he got more bullets he came back and finished off the jerries. PFC Milton Rosen lay wounded in face, shoulders, and legs. Nearly unconscious, he felt a German trying to tug off his boots. He shouted, "Get the hell away from here!"

And for some reason that Rosen would never understand, the German did exactly that.

PFC Elvis Cameron was found dead, with his hands around the neck of a dead German. Private Gideon Salmon, who had been recruited from the kitchen staff because of a shortage of men, killed one German, wounded another in the chest and shot the leg off a third. He could see the torn, bloody stump. The German shouted, *Verdamnter schwartzer!*"; and Gideon, who knew the words, let him live in pain and had to be stopped from shooting the bastard's other leg off.

Private Dave Ellis went to sleep in his foxhole when the attack was at its fiercest and woke up to find that somebody had covered his face with a crossword puzzle out of *Stars and Stripes*. Since his only hobby was the creation of obscene crossword puzzles, he concluded that a malicious friend had given him the treatment.

Only two other comic incidents are known to have taken place at the Battle of Perrier. One of them involved Private Olaf Gundersen, who duelled a drunken German with bottles of wine held like swords in an Errol Flynn movie—and lived to tell the tale. So did the German, who embraced the wine-soused Swede before being taken away to captivity.

The other incident happened to Captain West.

Now there were as many opinions about West as there were soldiers under him. A good fighter and a bad one, a brave man and a coward, a good planner and an inefficient one, a man who stood up for his subordinates and who threw them onto the stick; West was all things to all soldiers. But nobody ever denied that he had some sense of humor, and what happened at Perrier made a story on which he would dine out for the rest of his life. Hostesses would murmur at a lull in some party, "You must tell us what happened that time in France."

And West, who had played his part throughout a difficult time, in Africa and Italy, France and Germany and for a few weeks in Japan, and had seen living and dying, would know instantly what was wanted and would perform his little recitation. (Indeed, it is said that Ambassador West's anecdote beguiled the late President Kennedy so much before a meeting with Kruschev as to make him late; and when Kruschev was told the reason he countered with some beguiling World War Two anecdotes of his own.)

West was in the battle at night when the sky was lit fitfully with flares. The captain had lost his aide and was looking around irritably for him. A GI holding his M-1 shakily appeared out of the gloom. West knew he was a GI because of the way he talked. Flares or not, the captain couldn't see worth a damn.

"Okay, Adolf, here you go," the soldier said, ready to kill.

"This is Captain West." He spoke quietly. Nobody ever seriously faulted him with a lack of courage.

"Yeh? How do I know you aren't some slick con artist that Adolf sent over now that it's night?" the soldier demanded reasonably. "If you're really GI let me ask you one question and see what you know about

America. Two questions, actually."

"Just a damn minute," West started angrily.

"Shut your hole unless you're spoken to. Number one: what state do you come from?"

There was no point in arguing. "New York."

"Oh. Well, all right. If you're an American, Adolf, tell me what's the capital of New York State. *Quick!*"

"Albany," West said promptly.

That was when the soldier carved himself a place in the annals of the Third for all time. By a flare's light, West saw him raise the M-1 higher in a threatening way.

"You're wrong, Adolf," the GI said. "The capital of New York State is Buffalo."

To this day, nobody in the Third has any idea how Captain West saved his life. Probably the aide he'd been looking for just happened to get there in the nick of time. The oddest thing about the whole story was that it was repeated in hopes of making the men laugh, but they only chuckled sourly. Any one of them might have been that bugged-up GI.

17

Jeff had been back at base for some six hours along with the rest of Baker Company, when he became aware of the fact that Ryder wasn't anywhere around. Ryder had survived the attack and claimed he had accounted for half a dozen krauts before the others faded away and left their dead; with the top brass, Ryder knew very well that an army whose members left its dead behind with no effort to retreive them was an army in trouble. They might win engagements here and there—even inflict heavy casualties—but they were on an irreversible path to defeat.

When Baker got back, Ryder caught up on his sleep before being called to Lieutenant Hearn's presence.

"What's up?" Jeff asked when he saw his friend shortly afterwards. "Are you getting a punishment detail?"

"Not unless you call a recon job some kind of punishment."

"What are you reconning?"

With a complete disregard for security, Ryder said, "Adolf's gone underground in the vicinity, and we haven't got the location. Hearn finally decided it was time to send the best man in the outfit."

"Can't the F.F.I. give us any information?"

"They haven't, so far."

"If that's the case, what makes anybody in his right mind think *you* can find it?"

"Uncle Gil is the best, lad. It's that simple."

"You're damn good," Jeff agreed fervently, "and you'll die pretty damn efficiently if Adolf catches up with you."

"He won't."

Jeff wheeled around and left. He went to see Lieutenant Hearn, explaining that Ryder had saved his bacon more than once and he wouldn't want to feel that Ryder was in a spot where he couldn't do the same for him.

"Son, I sympathize," Hearn said, "but Ryder is going out on his lonesome this time."

Jeff would never have expected the supercautious Jeffrey Parton to do what he did next. He prepared his own field pack after Ryder had left, and made a point of following from a distance of fifty feet. He didn't think Ryder spotted him as the man left base and walked into the area that looked like Central Park back in New York City. Jeff never remembered what explanation he gave the MPs in order to get out, but it must have been effective. His heart had never beaten faster.

He was walking quietly from the back of one tree to the back of another when he stopped hearing Ryder's footsteps. Cautiously as ever, looking for traces of enemy with every step, Jeff went forward. Thick foliage led to a tree-lined clearing where Ryder stood grinning at him.

"You're AWOL, Part. Go back."

"On a job like this, fellow, you need somebody."

"I'll be all right."

"If Adolf catches you, he'll eat your ass."

Ryder looked him up and down, measuring him.

"You're a damn fool."

"Uh-huh."

"You don't really owe me anything."

"Aren't we wasting time aound here?"

Ryder nodded, then quietly told him to get moving. Jeff hadn't expected to be thanked, and wasn't surprised.

It was a trek he'd remember for a long time. That lost-in-Central-Park feeling remained strong, with unexpected pleasures here and there: oddly-shaped trees, cheeping birds, crickets, and a smell of warmth that explained why some men would only live on a farm. All through the search for a Nazi outpost, Jeff held his own. Ryder never had to make any ciritcisms of what Jeff was doing.

They stopped to eat, sitting on twin rocks, Ryder looking at some insect that he claimed resembled an octopus reduced to an inch in height. Jeff ate his rations carefully, saving a little for a snack later on.

Ryder, who had wolfed down everything, said something about a friend who had been killed back at Perrier. Then he shrugged, looked back at the foxholes they had dug in case of need, and got up.

"Move it and shake it, Part."

A concealed trail hidden by a canopy of giant trees was followed long enough to convince them that it led to nothing except a stream. An odor that he knew much too well struck Jeff's nostrils as he turned away. A dead man was close by.

Ryder, who must have caught the same horrid smell, stopped and parted half a dozen strands of man-high grass. Both men were able to see into an area not much larger than a sofa, where a dead man lay.

Keeping an eye out for trouble, Jeff saw enough to make him wish he had looked in some other direction. The dead man had been stripped, saturated with gas, and set on fire. The smell of gas had faded, but the smell of death was strong. He would always remember France with the smells of death, bodies rotting, excrement nearby, staring eyes, insects buzzing around the summertime corpses. *La belle* France, as far as he was concerned.

Parting the man-high grass must have set up a crude warning system. A soft slurring sound made him turn, M-1 at the ready, but he was too late; and so was Ryder. The split-second failure of alertness could be fatal, and it was the first time Jeff had ever known Ryder to be even a little slow.

Three Germans had come out of the underbrush—scruffy, dirty men in dirty uniforms, men smelling of vinegar. Each man carried a rifle, and one carried a knife in his teeth.

The German who approached Ryder found himself in a fight. Ryder landed two punches before another German carrying a thick rope chunked him behind the ear. Jeff couldn't possibly have taken a hand quickly enough, and didn't have any choice except to watch.

Ryder, unconscious, was trussed with the rope. A section was cut off with the knife, and Jeff was tied up with part of what remained. The rope smelled as if it had been dipped in vinegar and then coated with tar.

Ryder was slapped back to consciousness and forced on to his feet. His look at Jeff was made up of embarrassment and apology. Jeff, who had never seen his buddy in an apologetic mood, couldn't help wishing he had looked the other way.

He knew that they were going to be led to the company headquarters for which they had come looking. The only change in plans was that they'd be going there as prisoners.

They couldn't move well if they were trussed like

chickens, so the Nazis settled for tying their hands with sturdy green cord. At night they were tied hand and foot to a pair of trees, and untied long enough to eat dried bread with one hand—usually laced with snails or caterpillars—and to drink water that tasted less like wine than any that Jeff had known in this country.

When they were finished and had been tied again, the Germans settled down for some sleep. One guard stayed awake to watch them. Ryder didn't hesitate to talk.

"The Nazis are a bunch of mother-frigging bastards," Ryder said, and looked in back of him. By moon's light, the guard's stolid features hadn't changed expression.

"No spikka the English," Ryder said. "At least, not the general over there."

"Why are they taking us anyplace? Why didn't they kill us?"

"They want to ask questions, then kill us. Or want their superiors to do the asking."

"Nothing else makes sense." Jeff agreed reluctantly.

His own ropes were tied too securely for him to have the slightest chance of getting out of them. He relaxed as best he could.

"If we talk," he started.

"We will." Ryder spoke quickly. "No sense in phoney hero stuff. They're stronger and meaner. If they want us to talk, that's what we'll do."

"And they'll kill us afterwards, I suppose."

"Sure they will, the bastards." Ryder added calmly—"if they get the chance. Don't look so goddam excited, you jerk!"

"All right. What's going to stop them torturing us and then killing?"

"Getting out of here."

"How can we do that?"

"I'll handle the worst part. You just wait till I say 'now,' and then you get to work. Am I clear?"

"Almost."

"Jesus H. Christ, what's wrong?"

"We still don't know where the base is, where they operate out of."

"*I* know," Ryder said calmly. "One of the bastards mentioned which two towns it's between." Ryder sighed. "Get as much rest as you can, pal. In the morning we make our add-ee-yoos."

Jeff hesitated, trying to decide how he should suggest that Ryder give him the necessary information, in case something unforeseen happened. Ryder didn't seem to have considered the possibility.

Ryder fell asleep while Jeff was still trying to pick the right words. Jeff slept fitfully and spent more time awake. Ryder, he noticed, snored serenely.

As soon as he woke up, Jeff remembered that Ryder had made up his mind on an escape attempt this morning and that it could be the last that anybody ever saw of either soldier.

A guard untied Ryder, who was then gestured off to one side, not far from where the rifles were kept. Another guard was holding a rifle aimed at him, one of those cheap items the Germans were putting out these days. The third guard approached Jeff, who was almost untied when he saw Ryder's taut glance in his direction. Ryder must have been sure this was going to be the last chance for an escape; if they let themselves get tied up again they would be at the base before another day was over and never again be able to move against the Nazis.

Ryder shouted, "Now!" and pushed the man in front of him against the rifle-carrying guard. Jeff kicked the guard who'd been untying him. The kick landed in the guard's crotch, and he screamed and doubled over.

Jeff started for the bush, noticing out of the corner of an eye that Ryder's guards were confused as they cursed and shouted. Then Ryder did something Jeff would always think of as insane. He could have run towards the brush and joined Jeff in taking chances on a trek back without weapons, but he had decided to ease his chances and Jeff's. He stopped and reached arrogantly for one of the cheap rifles, then whirled around to make for the brush.

His grip on the rifle was secure, but the pause had given one of the guards time enough to get back his balance. He reached for a knife in his holster, the steel blade flashing in air. Ryder's brisk response sent the man doubling up with a bullet inside him.

Jeff ran at full speed, but for once Ryder didn't keep up with him. When he turned he saw Ryder holding the rifle with one hand with the palm of his other hand clamped against a body section between heart and stomach. The fingers of his left hand were reddening.

Jeff decided that they had put enough distance between themselves and the Germans to justify a short pause.

"You're not hit bad, are you?"

He wanted Ryder to laugh it off, but his friend didn't say a word. Now that Jeff came to notice it, Ryder's face had become gray.

"I pulled out the . . . sticker." He drew a deep breath. "Listen, you ought to know where Adolf's base is, just in case a miracle-in-reverse happens and I—well, I get sidetracked. The base is betw—"

"I don't want to hear," Jeff insisted. "You tell Hearn about it and not me."

"Do what I say and listen."

"No!" Jeff childishly put both hands firmly over his ears.

Ryder hit the crook of Jeff's right elbow with the tip of the ill-made rifle which had inflicted his wound.

"The base is between Rouge and Kalik," Ryder said carefully. "Near Amiens, I think. Territory we captured pretty recently, so that Adolf can work from behind the lines."

"I've forgotten those names already. We ought to get a move on and haul some ass if we don't want those bastards finding us again."

It was the first time he had taken the initiative in suggesting some movement, and he wished he hadn't felt the need.

He hadn't taken more than half a dozen running steps before he knew that Ryder was in trouble again. Jeff took his rifle away, then put an arm around him and tried to walk quickly instead of running. He knew perfectly well that it was dangerous, but there wasn't any other way to handle it unless he . . .

No, he wouldn't do that. Damn it, no!

Ryder suddenly lurched forward and out of Jeff's reach, falling face down.

Jeff's first move was to turn him onto his back. Sweatdrops had started to line the backs of Jeff's hands, and he wiped them furiously against his uniform.

Jeff pulled Ryder's red-stained hand away from the wound, which was close to the heart. It was what Jeff had been afraid of.

"Go ahead," Ryder said. "I'll be—all right."

"I can wait till you're ready."

"Don't be a shmuck!" Ryder couldn't talk clearly, and Jeff had to strain forward to catch the words. "Run like hell, and keep a tight asshole."

"If the krauts find you, they'll make your life hell and then kill you."

"Kid, if you want to keep me from getting found by old Adolf, there's only one way."

"Don't talk like that!"

"I'm not shitting you, kid." Ryder forced his lips to make what he may have considered a smile. "Let's see how much of a GI you really are, Part."

"You don't want me to do that," Jeff whispered.

Ryder's smile this time was a little more genuine. "I wouldn't want anybody doing it who wasn't a buddy."

Jeff wanted to make his mind blank, but he was still soldier enough to repeat the information he had been given a few minutes ago, to let Ryder feel some assurance about that.

He couldn't see too well because what was in front of him had become blurry and wet. He reached for the cheap rifle and put one end of it against Ryder's head. He pulled the trigger.

The lower part of Ryder's face was still intact. Jeff bent over and kissed the lips in that hideous half-face, then staggered to his feet and began running blindly.

He never remembered many details about what happened during the next couple of days. After a while he slowed down and went back to walking. There wasn't any food left, and it was impossible to forage around. Above all, he wouldn't think about what had happened back there. *He wouldn't think about it.*

He looked at grass and trees, at a hundred and one different forms of screeching, slithering, sitting, cawing, pecking, rustling, placid, angry life. There was life everywhere except in . . .

He woudn't think about it.

Jeff must have done plenty of walking in the night, too. Whether or not he was moving in circles, he didn't know. He had made up his mind to guide himself by the North Star, but didn't see it in the sky. He was afraid to tell himself the truth—that for practically the first time in his life Jeffrey Parton didn't know what he was doing or why.

By the second day he was nearly out of his head. He started shouting:

"Ryder, Ryder, Ryder!"

Always three times, then a pause, and then the same shout again.

He might have spent much longer being lost if not for a well-disguised piece of good fortune. On the afternoon of the second day he twisted an ankle on a chunk of rock and fell headlong through the brush and into a rough clearing.

A civilian stood there, gaping at him, and speaking French. He came closer, drew back, shouted. A bushy man appeared quickly, glanced down at Jeff, and ran in another direction. Carefully, Jeff got to his feet, grimacing. When the second man came back he was followed by a man in a deep blue Free French uniform. Jeff had never been so glad to see anyone in his life.

"American? You're not too far from home. I'll arrange for friendly hands to get you there."

The Frenchman wasn't surprised to see the Yank burst out crying. He assumed it was because the American felt safe for the first time in days. The Frenchman never found out the real reason for Jeff's scalding tears, but after a few minutes he might have guessed. He had been fighting for a while himself.

Jeff reached the base in a marketing truck and on an improvised stretcher. Late in the afternoon he was taken to the base hospital. Peppery Dr. Fortune examined him, concernedly at first, raffishly amused afterwards. One of the medics bandaged him. He'd have to spend the better part of a week in the hospital, but he was a damn lucky GI if ever there was one.

The war was going well. The Germans were giving up territory to which they'd had no right in the first place. They were falling back, but taking casualties and inflicting them as well. There didn't seem any doubt that the tide was turning decisively against the Germans; it was only a matter of trying to keep them from destroying the whole world first.

Lieutenant Hearn didn't take such a rosy view of Jeff's good fortune. Hearn came running to the base hospital as soon as he was told that Parton had shown up. His young face was set in grim lines.

"AWOL is nothing to gag about," he told Jeff.

"I can tell you where the German base is, sir," Jeff did.

Hearn left the hospital room without another word. Half an hour later he came back and settled down calmly. "How'd you get this information?"

Jeff told him.

"What happened to Ryder?"

Jeff told that part of it, too.

"A bad business, soldier," Hearn said. "I'll see if I can keep you from a prison stretch and a dishonorable discharge. I don't have to tell Doctor Fortune to try and keep you from suicide—do I?"

"No, sir."

"Good. Besides, you'll miss the U.S.O. show in a couple of days. Jack Benny, I think it is."

Hearn winked at him and walked out.

Two days of agonizing uncertainty went past before Jeff saw the lieutenant again. It was impossible to tell from looking at him whether Hearn was bringing good news or the other kind.

"Parton, you'll be glad to hear that a full-scale attack has been mounted on the kraut base near Amiens, and so far it looks like a winner."

"Is Baker in this, sir?"

'No. We took heavy casualties at Perrier, and replacement haven't come in from the repple-depple. Not yet."

"I see, sir."

"As you completed a dangerous mission with skill and success, Parton, you've been made a corporal."

"Thank you, sir."

"Don't be in a hurry to thank me, Parton. Because you left on that mission without specific orders, you're being busted back to private. In fact, you're right back where you started from. Your pal, Ryder, was always getting promoted and busted, too, according to our records. I guess you two have a lot in common at that."

"My friend . . . ." Jeff's face twisted, and he turned to the wall rather than look at Hearn any more. The lieutenant said he'd tell Doc Fortune to keep an eye on Jeff after all, every once in a while. Just to see how Jeff was holding up.

18

"Listen here, son," Dr. Fortune said irritably. "You couldn't do anything but what you did about your friend and we both know it. Keep skulling over it and you'll crack the hell up."

"How can I keep from going back over it?"

And Fortune said softly, "The people who crack up are the ones who never learned to forgive themselves. Maybe it's the last lesson you have to learn, the last one that the Army can teach you."

"How do I learn it?" Jeff asked carefully.

"By forgiving somebody else," Fortune said. "Forgive Ryder for having been wounded and yourself for not having been able to save him."

"He saved me a million times, and when I had a chance to do something for him I didn't."

"Nobody could have, from what you say."

"But I *had* to." Jeff hit a fist against the kneecap of his good leg, then winced and shut his eyes tightly.

"I've got nothing more to say," Fortune told him. "Maybe God will be good to you, son, and let you learn."

The soldier in the bed next to Jeff's was named Isaac Berg and known as Iz. He had lost an arm to a German mine on patrol with Delta Company, and his bitterness was painful to see. He would sit glowering for hours, and hardly made any remarks except nasty ones. He hated the hospital, the doctors, the army, the Nazis, the Japs, the other American soldiers, sailors, marines, and coast guardsmen. He never told anybody what career he expected to take up when he became a civilian once again, but made it clear that the loss of an arm had ruined his chances at it.

The GIs who were more used to their troubles called him "Sunshine." When another soldier with two good arms called him "you kike bastard," Iz pounded that other GI into a state of near unconsciousness. Dr. Fortune referred to him as GAM, or God's Angry Man.

No part of the hospital program won Iz's scorn more than the therapy sessions. He made a point of doing absolutely nothing and couldn't be talked or threatened into changing his mind.

He was at least considerate enough to keep quiet when he and the other ambulatory patients got together in the auditorium below ground to see a movie. He muttered under his breath at such goodies as *Bataan* and *Back to Bataan*, wondering why the Army was always showing movies about soldiers. A light picture called *Navy Blues* caused him to turn the air blue with profanity, but only afterwards. And he cried at a light comedy called *Appointment for Love* because he thought that Margaret Sullavan was so beautiful and she'd never look at him.

He never complained during live entertainment, when famous comedians from the States told jokes and pretty girls sang to organ accompaniment. He hardly ever talked about it afterwards, as the others did.

It happened that a girl singer named Fan Meggit was visiting the base. Fan was rated as highly as Ella Fitzgerald or Doris Day or Helen O'Connell among band singers. Before leaving for her next stop, she did a show for the patients. Iz sat glowering in bed, wanting to avoid the sight of a beautiful girl.

It turned out that Fan Meggit was only pretty, nothing more. All the same it was too much. She went from room to room for the patients who couldn't get up to see her show. The men in their beds applauded vigorously. Iz glared at those men in the big barn of a room, the men using both hands. Jeff was on the verge of shouting angrily. If Fan Meggit hadn't been so nice in a fresh-faced Doris-Day manner, he probably would have done just that.

Fan launched into a trio of standards, then announced a new song that she felt sure would become a hit. It was called, *When I'm in Your Loving Arms.*

Jeff looked quickly over toward Iz, ready to take any necessary steps to keep the guy quiet. Iz's face had turned a deep red, but he didn't say anything. As Jeff watched in amazement, Iz covered himself to the neck.

Fan Meggit bowed low when the song was over, causing some extra whistles and a torrent of applause. She was wearing a low-cut evening dress that showed her off in a very effective way. Walking from one bed to another, shaking hands when she could, the vision spoke trivial and foolish words. But the voice belonged to a pretty girl wearing perfume, a girl with sleek blonde hair, so that the men were in a state of mind bordering on hypnosis.

She offered to take a message to Jeff's parents or girl friend or both. Jeff, who was afraid he might be imposing, thanked her but said that it wasn't necessary.

Iz made himself smile at her, which surprised Jeff

more than anything he had seen in months. Fan repeated her offer to take a message, and held her hand poised over a notebook. Iz shook his head and forgot to thank her—or else he was too involved with his own feelings to go that far. Fan Meggit wished him luck and went on to the next soldier.

Jeff turned to Iz as soon as she was gone, eyes bulging with disbelief. "If I hadn't seen it I'd never have believed it," he said. "Of all people, Iz, why didn't you let her have the works? You know, let her see the stump so she could feel miserable. Hell, you even covered yourself when she started to sing the goddam song."

"Forget it," Iz said.

"Hell, no! you can't blame a guy for being curious."

Iz groped for the explanation. "Well, I could 'a done it, but she came out here and offered to take messages, so I guess she meant well." Iz shrugged, returning if only briefly to his usual manner. "Can she help it if she's a stupid, tactless bitch?"

Jeff's own attitude started to improve after he saw Iz Berg forgive Fan Meggit for her unintentional foolishness. Six weeks had passed since he had written to his girl back home. In his next letter he told Marilyn bluntly that it wouldn't be fair to her if she waited for him without seeing anybody else, adding that there was no definite arrangement between them.

A powerful desire to call that letter back came upon him once it was out of his hands. Was it possible that

Marilyn didn't want to go out with any other guys because she loved him? Did he feel the same way about her? Maybe she *was* the girl he'd marry when he got back.

If he got back.

He decided against sending a follow-up letter so quickly. In a few weeks he'd let her know that he did feel strongly about her, but remained convinced that he had no right to tie her up emotionally. Odd that he hadn't realized how he genuinely felt about the girl until he wrote one fairly honest letter—but he was glad he'd figured it out at last.

He wrote a letter to his parents, too, but in that one he said very little. It amazed him that he could fill up two pages, and supposed he wouldn't have gone through with it except for knowing that the folks were anxious to hear from him.

Mort Kaplan had brought him the address of Ryder's married sister, and he wrote her a letter as well. He wanted to tell her that he missed Ryder, his best friend in the Army, the one who had taught him so many things—and taught him in the process how to become more of a man than the Jeff Parton who had been drafted only a few months ago.

But the right words wouldn't come. He spent the better part of a day trying to get that letter the way he wanted it, but what came out were phrases that didn't convey anything special about his friend. Finally he put the damn thing aside, came back to it, finished it quickly and sent it off. He had known that Ryder hadn't gotten along well with anybody in his family and wasn't surprised when he never got any answer from the woman.

19

The hospital interlude, which had originally been supposed to last one week, took six of them. Before he was much older, Jeff would know that doctors always seemed to be predicting short stays that ended up as long ones.

He spent a little time in a newly liberated town, engaged in honorable drinking. From now on, he was going to be like Anse Tarves, talking to some guys and doing favors that made sense, not turning his back on anybody who was in this mess with him. But on the other hand he didn't have the slightest intention of making another close friend—not even one. He'd had enough of that. Make a pal in this war and you could lose him next day. Give any part of yourself and it got cut off by a grenade, a frag bomb, a mine. Instead, he would be a loner from now on.

That sensible and cautious decision would have been worthy of Jeff Parton *before* he got into the Army.

One Thursday morning he was back with the squad and waiting to be sent forward. A gin rummy game was going on. Sergeant O'Caffie watched the whole business with a fatherly eye, walking from hand to hand and make appropriate facial expressions until he caught Mort Kaplan watching him shrewdly.

A clean-faced kid walked into the dugout that was the scene of the game, looked around him and walked over to O'Caffie. The Sergeant looked surprised and then drew out a hand.

A ghastly suspicion pinked Jeff. "What in hell do *you* want here?" he demanded.

"I'm new."

"*You*? They sent you here to take the place of Gil Ryder?"

"I don't know who I'm replacing."

Jeff had got up from the impromptu table and was wrenching the young soldier's arm.

Back of him, O'Caffie said calmly, "Let the kid go, Part."

Jeff did it slowly, but was making and unmaking fists as he stood in place.

"What have you got against Indelli, Part?"

"This jerky kid shouldn't be near anything that Gil Ryder ever heard of. He isn't a GI, he's a piece of crap. He isn't good enough to kiss Ryder's ass, and I don't want to look around to see what they sent here to take Gil's place."

"You don't want!" O'Caffie spoke tonelessly. "It's nice to know that somebody is running the whole goddam army from one lousy dugout."

"For Christ's sweet sake, Sergeant! Don't you know what I'm taking about?"

"Sure I do. You think you're in charge of preserving Gil Ryder's memory. You and nobody else."

"All I want is—"

"What you want is impossible, Part. This kid is named Jack Indelli and he takes Ryder's place so we can have a full squad. Any questions?"

"All right, Sergeant, I guess I was out of line there for a minute. I don't really care what happens around here any more, so long as I get left alone."

"I can't oblige you on that, either."

"At least I don't want to see this piece of crap close to me."

"Sorry, Parton."

"What does *that* mean?"

"Well, now, you're a little pissed off because Indelli is taking Gil Ryder's place and Ryder was your buddy."

"He was a lot more than that," Jeff flared.

"Okay, Part, but hear me out. I can remember back to when Ryder himself was p.o.'d because you were taking the place of his own best buddy, Burris Barnes. Do you remember that, Part? Well? You're pretty damn quiet all of a sudden."

"I remember it," Jeff muttered.

"All right. Ryder was the best man in the squad, and I told him to clue you in on whatever you didn't know." The sergeant paused. "It cured him, Part, after a while. And for all I know, the same cure could work again."

"Now just a damn minute, Sergeant," Jeff began.

"It's an order, Part," O'Caffie said bluntly. "The kid needs a rabbi, and you're him."

"I won't do it."

"Do you want charges instead?"

Jack Indelli asked quietly, "Can't you assign me to somebody else, Sergeant? Please? There won't be anything but trouble, otherwise."

"Shut up, son," O'Caffie said to him. "Well, Part?"

"The hell with it, Sergeant."

O'Caffie smiled and said, "You can let off as much steam as you want to if it makes you feel better. Ryder did that, too. But you be ready to show this kid the ropes when the time comes, and you keep an eye on him. I don't expect to tell you this stuff all over again."

Jeff nodded once.

20

A company can be wiped out as a whole striking force, but remnants are usually left over to become damned dangerous to the enemy. The German companies that had been wiped out as units still retained soldiers and mortars and crews and food and medical supplies. To use what was left in the most effective way, some German officers decided to smash one village before the U.S. Army's rebuilding program could finish its task.

The attack was mounted from a point beyond the village perimeter, of course, and carried out on the night that a newly augmented Baker Company took its place on night patrol duty. The first mortar sheel landed on the newly built orphanage. Then a succession of mortar rounds rocked the village.

The newly-moved-forward CP bought it, blowing up with half a dozen inside. Only one escaped, PFC Percy Montrose, running out of that flaming cabin with two belts of ammo in each hand. He belly-flopped to keep his body away from the debris, but couldn't protect himself when the communications center blew up next to him. He lay groaning for minutes, the unused bullet belts in his hands. Then he stopped groaning and was still.

Moments before that shell hit, Avery Varian started sending an "Immediate Operation" message. He might have got more of it through if he had lived.

Sergeant Anthony Innaurato called for flares to be fired instantly from the mortar pits. The illumination was desperately needed, of course, but it lit the way for a shell that killed him immediately.

A number of locals had come running out of their homes, shouting in terror. With the help of seven of them, Sergeant O'Caffie began pulling papers and med supplies out of what was left of the CP building, and dragging out weapons and ammo for the mortar pits.

The men of Baker Company hurried out to battle. Private Harmon Shadegg, for instance, carried a grenade moments after the pin had been pulled out and mercifully dropped it before the damn thing exploded when he was a hundred feet off.

The two medics, involved in a rescue, were blasted by mortar shells, and hit so badly that no one could identify either man except by dog tag.

Jeff Parton had rounded up a number of villagers and taken them to safety—or a least to a point far beyond immediate action. The kid, Indelli, tried to help, but Jeff told himself he was too busy even to talk to him, let alone instruct him. Mortar shells lit the air, but not as well as flares.

Six able-bodied villagers and a woman named Madeleine had volunteered to help. They were put in charge of evacuating other villagers to safety, and did it well. The girl, particularly, distinguished herself.

PFC Robert Clapper was shot in the right hand, making it useless. He ran over to PFC Hubert Mustin, whose left hand was out of commission. They worked together, one man taking the pins out of grenades for the other to throw.

When PFC Gene Carr was wounded, his buddy Dirk Dickson tore up a shirt to help stanch the bleeding. The shirt was practically shoved in Carr's wound, but didn't do the trick. Dickson put an arm around his buddy and started for the closest foxhole. A deadly accurate machine-gun burst cut down both of them.

Then Indelli called, "Medic! Medic!"

He brought a burst of gun fire down on himself and Jeff Parton. Jeff ducked into a mortar pit, waiting for it to be over, and Indelli followed quickly.

Jeff said, "Stupid, you talk English out loud and Adolf will hammer at you."

"What should I say?"

"Call out to the nearest soldier, just loud enough, that there's a wounded man nearby. That one will call in turn. A medic will get over, if it's at all possible."

The mortar pit wasn't active. Jeff stationed Indelli in the middle and paced back and forth, firing at random in the chaos and hoping to convince the Germans that more than two men were in the mortar pit. Over his head an illuminating flare was trailed by a shine of white phosphorous.

But it was the illumination given off by an enemy grenade that permitted O'Caffie to see the Germans coming toward the camp, already in the area of the outer perimenter. The outpost had certainly been overrun by this time.

The German who first got to the cover was riddled with bullets, but the one who followed and used his dead comrade as a screen did manage to get past the barbed wire and back of the line.

PFC Tom Short saw a pair of Germans closing in on one of the mortar pits at the village perimeter. He had been carrying an automatic in a holster, and now he used it. One of the Germans screamed, and Short saw his face drenched in blood. The other fell after the second shot, both hands at his neck.

Over the deadly small arms fire Sergeant Clarence

Bohun could hear sounds of fierce struggle. He whirled to his left, where a village woman struggled with all her might against a powerful uniformed intruder. Rather than take a chance on the woman being hurt, Bohun planned to use his gun as a policeman's nightstick. The intruder suddenly whirled, carrying the woman's body with him. He fired pointblank, smashing Bohun's left leg below the kneecap. Bohun found the strength—it was probably pure reflex—to fire back instantly, and saved his life. The infiltrator fell, taking the screaming woman down with him.

At that moment a civilian who had been with the woman before the attack started running forward, shouting and cursing and waving his fists in the air. The civilian offered too good a target for any German sharpshooter to miss. He was hit three times and fell without making a sound. The woman lay under that dead man's body, praying for the murderous fire to ease up and give her a chance to crawl away.

Mort Kaplan was in a foxhole when he saw two krauts with submachine guns. He knew that both of the guns were pointed at him and that he was probably going to meet his maker in a short time. He raised his M-1 to take at least one of the Germans with him. A mortar shell exploded at a point between himself and the infiltrator, sending Mort high up into the air. He landed five feet off, dazed and shaken, but the infiltrators had been killed by their own side's shell and Mort was still alive.

Sergeant O'Caffje was directing use of the flares, hoping that they'd light up the area till help could arrive. When a German infiltrator showed up, submachine gun in hand, O'Caffie pulled out an automatic from his holster and shot the man dead. He tried to grab for the damn thing, but another German got it first and would have fired at O'Caffie if the gun hadn't jammed. O'Caffie finished him off. The submachine gun was no good, so he threw the damn thing into the darkness and listened with pleasure as somebody called out in German with obvious surprise and delight. The weapon didn't help that one, either. He was soon dead.

Jack Indelli got his first shot at a German whose location had been pinpointed by an illumination flare. Even as he squeezed off the shot, Indelli knew he had missed. The German had been raising a hand to throw a grenade, and the bullet struck that grenade. It blew the enemy to pieces as Indelli wached. He didn't have time to become sick at the sight; another German had appeared and there was no time to indulge himself. He thought he saw Parton nod at the sight of that first enemy blowing up, but couldn't be sure.

Tom Granit, the soft-spoken Southern BAR man, had been caught by the attack near the QM supply depot. He was able to run out. In the dark he collided with another soldier. As they staggered away from each other, a flare lighted up that soldier's face, and Granit was looking at Anse Tarves.

"What are you doing here?" he said, not pausing to guess that Tarves had been given a gun because of a shortage of men, which often happened to blacks in the kitchen area at times of need. "Out of my way, boy!"

Tarves had been sighting a German, but now he refused to move an inch and tried to push Granit out of his way. The infiltrator's number-one grenade finished off both of them.

O'Caffie, who had seen what happened and came upon the bodies moments afterward, saw Mort Kaplan looking at the two dead men and muttering something in Hebrew.

O'Caffie said, "If they hadn't hated each other

such a hell of a lot, they'd probably still be alive. Don't waste sympathy on either of them.''

In spite of the din, medical sergeant Martin Lawes' hands never shook as he applied dressings. While one man was getting emergency treatment, a buddy held his head to help ease the pain. He looke up angrily when Sergeant O'Caffie shouted for him to get busy at one of the mortar pits, but stood up and ran. The wounded soldier groaned as his buddy ran off, then bit his lip.

Illumination flares were working two ways, of course, giving both the Germans and the men of Baker Company light that was needed for killing. It was odd, too, how small noises could be made out despite the thunder of guns.

At one point Sylvan Watkins took into his head to call out, "For Christ's sake, stop scratching yourself like that!"

Private Maclean Dugger suddenly shouted that he was deaf and couldn't hear a thing. He didn't hear the bullet that his words drew to him, either, and died instantly.

Chrétien Durand, one of the villagers, ran out of a house in which he had been hiding and picked up rocks which he started to hurl at the invaders. He picked off one German and took his grenades. Every one that was thrown turned out to be a dud. The only exception was the masher that blew up Private Hary Aitken's eyes, killing him. Durand went back to using rocks.

Sergeant O'Caffie was on his way toward one of the mortar pits when he felt a sudden twinge of pain. Looking down at himself, he realized that he had been touched by a wedge of shrapnel. His right foot was bleeding. He ignored it and hurried on his way, shouting orders at the men. When he decided to hold off for a minute, he ripped part of his shirt off and used it to make a tight bandage. *The damn thing had better hold*, he said to himself, and went back to work.

He found Sergeant Basil Tryanor with a med and asked, "Do you know where Hearn is?"

"The lieutenant?" Traynor could only get out his words with difficulty. "He bought it. The first or second blast creamed him."

For a moment O'Caffie closed his eyes tightly. Then he opened them wide, blinked rapidly, and ran out to where the trouble was. He supervised the dispersal of shells to the various pits.

Parton and Indelli were at one of these, firing at figures lit by various illuminating shells. Indelli was convinced that Parton wasn't hurting the enemy at all, but soon realized that Jeff was firing in such a way as to force the German attacker within range or other pits, where he could be sliced to pieces.

During a pause, Parton asked tiredly, "Do you still want some advice from me?"

"Yes, sure."

"Okay," Was Parton smiling? Had he remembered something now of all times? "My advice is to keep a tight asshole. That's my advice."

Indelli suddenly whirled. Jeff, following almost against his will, saw that a German had reached one of the ammo depots. Indelli picked him off, but the dying German dropped a grenade from his hand. The sound of so much ammo buying it at one time made every GI, no matter what he might have been doing at the time, suddenly reach up and hold his ears.

A small fire grew larger before anything could be done to stop it. The wind was with the Third this time, fire streaking off into the village. One hut after another caught it, blazing against the sky to light up the Germans' hiding places at the same time. Two dozen Germans died in the next two dozen minutes.

A mortar crew arrived at the pit that Jeff and Indelli had been using, a grim and jumpy group. Less than five minutes had passed since the attack had gotten under way.

A shell was picked up clumsily, and residue from a previous charge was cleaned out of the mortar. Jeff Parton let out a roar of frustration at the slow pace and pulled out the safety clip himself to set the timer. The crewmen eased that shell into muzzle.

"Give 'em one for Ryder!" Jeff shouted.

The shell was fired. Now the rhythm picked up, and the next shell was inside the muzzle in half the time it had taken for the first.

"And one for Burris Barnes!" Jeff shouted.

A shorter pause and then, "One for Anse Tarves!" and again, "One for Tom Granit!" and again, "One for Lieutenant Hearn!" and then, "One more for Ryder!" and "Another for Ryder!" And, "This one for Ryder, too!"

Jack Indelli, watching out of the corner of an eye while he fired at occasional moving figures in the darkness, told himself that Ryder must have been quite a fellow if even his memory and the sound of his name could be such an inspiration at a time like this. Why, Ryder might have been almost as good a GI as Jeff Parton.

The Battle went on, but conditions didn't favor the Germans so much by this time. The Third was in command of itself at last.

Sylvan Watkins closed hand-to-hand with a German and killed him by knocking him down and stamping on his neck. If he'd had ammo he'd have shot the man. As it was, he had to use the weapon that was handiest.

Some time after the battle was finished, Herbert Dickens' body was found in back of a skinny little tree at the tail end of the village. In spite of fire damage, it was plain that Dickens had been tortured. He had been tied with a rope that had been knotted and tightened around his forehead till his skull cracked. Jack Indelli happened to see the body, and the sight made him throw up his K-rations.

A well that had been dug by the army engineers permitted the villagers to form bucket brigades to put out the fire. They were surprisingly successful until a German mortar shell zeroed in on target and blasted the well to pieces, killing four Frenchmen.

In that deathly chaos of flashing light, screams, shot and shell, cut and thrust, and killing after killing, the sound of planes coming in relief could be heard clearly. Bombers and fighters rocked the enemy. Silver-spotted planes helped direct battery fire. Jeff happened to see a plane go down in flames that destroyed a bothersome enemy nest as it crashed.

When the Germans started to withdraw their scattered units, fighter planes were ordered to overfly so that the Germans would get the notion their escape was blocked.

Other planes dropped med supplies, food, and ammunition over the area. Men from Delta and Hotel Companies were dropped past the point where the Germans were on the run in hopes of leaving them nowhere to go and nothing to do but stand and fight it out.

"It can't hurt to keep your eye peeled," Jeff Parton told Indelli. "One German can still do a lot of damage."

They were on the way to the rear, hoping for a break that would last for as much as half an hour—if they were in luck.

Jeff was cupping the heels of his hands against his aching eardrums when he saw that Indelli looked miserable. The newcomer was sitting with his helmet between his feet and his head down almost to the knees. His eyes were tight shut and the corners of his lips turned down. Certainly he was feeling bitter and angry.

"What's wrong, kid?" Jeff asked softly. "Want your money back?"

Indelli looked up at this sharp and experienced soldier who couldn't have had many months on him in age or length of army service.

"How do you take this shit?" he asked.

"There's no choice."

"You're damned inhuman!"

"Hell, no! I have to do this job, and I go ahead with it. That's all there is to that. You're in the same boat."

"Will it ever get finished?"

"Wars get done sooner or later, they tell me. One side gets tired, and then it's all over."

"I still don't see how you can stomach this."

"Look, Indelli, you're going to keep saying I'm some kind of a pig, and I'm going to keep telling you that I haven't got any choice. We'll go around in circles for months."

"Don't you regret anything you've done out here?"

"Yes."

"For instance?"

"Drop that." Parton's voice was so strong that Indelli made up his mind not to carry the point further.

"I've been a horse's ass, haven't I?" he asked quietly. "Asking you a question like that one, for Christ's sake! That's not enough."

"What else?"

"Well, I just about set the village on fire."

Jeff Parton nearly smiled. "With a match?"

"You know what I mean. I cut into the German and he blew up everything in sight and the whole fire began."

"Nobody expected you to ask him politely to drop dead."

"But still and all—"

"Hell, you don't think it was you who should have done this thing. A lot of people figure that way about themselves. A thing has got to be done, but they don't want to be the ones who do it. Well, the ones who actually do the rough things figure the same way, but go ahead and do them because somebody has to. I guess that's the difference between most of the guys who make it out of here when their time is up and the ones who don't. Those who make it generally did something."

"I don't know how else I could have handled that German."

"If you'd been thinking a little clearer, you'd have

tried to shoot him in the head and paralyze him on the split second your bullet landed. The grenade wouldn't really have done that much actual damage."

"I suppose so. I'll try and do better next time."

"Sure, but something else will come up and you never were in a spot like that before. Either you'll blow your top the next time, too, or you'll be okay."

"My basic was pretty thorough."

"It doesn't get you set up for the idea that whatever happens out here is for real."

Indelli hesitated.

"What else is bugging you?" Jeff sounded short tempered, which was exactly the way he felt. "Puke it out and you'll feel a lot better."

"You said you didn't want anything to do with me. What made you change your mind?"

"The Sergeant."

'You could have thrown me to the wolves out there." He hesitated. "It can't be on account of my talking English too loud or indirectly starting the fire. Or killing the German."

"No, it isn't any of those things."

"When then? I think I've got a right to ask."

"I don't really know what to tell you. My best friend in the army, the guy who taught me everything, got stung pretty bad by the Germans. He—well, I had to make sure Adolf couldn't get him. Do you know what I mean?"

"I think so."

"After that happened, I swore I was going to play the Army real cool from then on. I wasn't going to let myself call any other guy a close friend. You've got to admit I was thinking in a sensible, practical way."

"What kept you from doing it?"

"Because a man can't really live like that in the Army—or anyplace else if you want to know the truth. I'm not sure you can live anywhere if you aren't part of somebody or something and you don't give of yourself." Jeff Parton paused. "If you ever tell anybody I talked like this, I'll knock your teeth out through your ass."

Sergeant O'Caffie was shouting to the others, "Come on, you lazy, stupid, gutless bastards. Get with it!"

As Jeff led the way back to the village perimeter, still keeping his eyes firmly fixed for any possible snipers, he said to Indelli, "You play gin rummy?"

"I'm pretty good at it."

"We'll see. Baker Company keeps a special gin rummy file."

Indelli laughed with relief, throwing his head back.

Jeff said sharply, "Don't do that when you're working. Keep your eyes peeled."

Indelli was startled. "Can't you relax for even a second?"

"Sure, if you want to raise the chances of being zapped."

"Oh."

"And when you go into a new town, look for kids. If you don't see any kids in sight, you're in trouble. If a few are in sight but they seem scared, you're in extra trouble. If the kids look friendly, then you *may* be all right."

"I see."

"And whatever routine you hit for moving around when you're close to action, don't take the same trail twice in a row or at the same time every day."

"Right."

"If you do any driving in France, you'd better speed up when you get to the crossroads. Want to know why? Otherwise if you put the brakes on when you're expected to, you might get a little lead note from Adolf."

Indelli nodded to show that he had understood.

"Anytime we have to clean out a bunker, I'll flip the masher in and walk ahead of you after the smoke clears. If you don't walk in my steps you might trip a wire and get yourself a load of shit between the eyes. Are you getting all this, Indelli?"

"Yes."

The course of instruction had officially started, with Jeff giving his hard-won information to another in hopes that it would help save one life and that Indelli would pass it on to somebody else—all the bits and pieces of trade talk that could make the difference as to whether a man came back.

The mopping-up work was hard, even for these well equipped men with barbed hand grenades and air support. It made the men feel better to know that more of them were here. If anything happened, a medic would get to you that much quicker—but knock on wood and pray to God it doesn't happen.

The mop-up cost the men from Delta and Hotel and Baker an extra seventy-five casualties, including twenty dead and the platoon members who caught it when the wind shifted and an American mortar shell struck them. Officially the casualties were listed as "moderate to heavy."

The Germans lost an extra three hundred men in

the mop-up, most of them wounded who were killed by other Germans to keep from getting caught. A remnant got away, though, and they'd be back somewhere to raise more hell.

The village would be built up properly this time. With luck, the Germans would leave it alone so that the natives could improve their conditions.

And the war? It would go on, with the Germans sending in other divisions to make up for those that had been chopped to pieces or taken prisoner. And the men of the Third never doubted that they'd chop these new enemies into hamburger, too.

21

Everybody knows that World War Two was fought for good and sufficient reasons, and most people think that the men who fought were noble and brave. It is accepted that the men who didn't come back died for a reason—not in vain.

And what happened to them when they came back was similar in some ways to what happened to the men from World War One. Oh, there wasn't a depression to contend with. And there was a GI bill that sent a lot of them to school and returned the government's money in the form of taxes because the graduates earned more and paid accordingly.

As for the war itself, they remembered the discomforts in a vague way, and the feeling of having been young was enough to put a hazy glow over almost everything else. In those days they could touch their toes without bending their knees, and every woman was an adventure—so the other things couldn't really have been too bad. And they hate every war without mercy—except the one they fought when they were young.

Every five years afterwards, the survivors of the company used to stage a reunion in some big hotel. The wives hadn't come at first because of the needs of their children, but later on they started coming between shopping trips and even found some reflected glory in being close to a war veteran who had seen action against a notably savage enemy in what everyone has called a good war.

The survivors noticed with vague regret that this one's hair is turning gray and that one's hair is falling out and the other one is getting fatter than hell.

Jeff Parton got married to his girl and went back to studying to be an accountant and made a good thing of it. Two of his three children have turned out pretty well, but the younger boy has had a spell of drug-taking and twice tried to kill himself. Jeff won't talk about that. He does allow himself to become a little mellow and talk about the old days, though.

"Remember that rappelling business?" he said at the bar while his wife was talking to some other women. "You know the way I learned? Well, you guys remember Gil Ryder." He looked a little grim, but the look faded and he kept talking. "Well, Ryder took me up in the goddam tree one time, and said he wasn't going to take any more foolishness from me. By God, he said, he was going to teach me right now. So he. . ."

Iz Berg, the onehanded soldier, had become a probation officer and seemed to laugh all the time. Married, with a daughter who had been married and divorced inside a twelve month period, Iz seemed the closest to being a happy man.

He asked, "Remember Nils Cardoness?"

"The writer? Sure. Were you there the night he bought it?"

"*Was I!*" Somebody else had spoken. "Boy, I was right in the group when Gil Ryder started organizing everything!"

Somebody else asked, "Did you guys ever hear the story about Mort Kaplan and the condom he got from Lieutenant Liddell?"

"No. What happened that time?"

Mort Kaplan was the joker of the reunion, making little remarks about his wife, his two children, and his ailments. Over the last years, what with diabetes and high blook pressure, they had become genuine.

Jack Indelli has married for money and gone into his father-in-law's business at the top. He drank more than most of the others and argued in public with his wife.

And everybody had stories to tell about the men who didn't make it back. There was the story about Avery Varian and the phony telegram he once rigged up for a soldier—Watkins, was it? And there was Anse Tarves, who used to sneak off to eat watermelon. Some of the men were always narrow-minded enough to miss the real point of that story. Some of the blacks who fought well in different sections appeared at the reunion, and there was a distinct edging away on both sides and vague promises to keep in touch before the next reunion. Those promises never meant anything, and everybody knew it.

Sergeant O'Caffie was always invited, but being Regular Army he didn't really belong at a get-together of citizen-soldiers. Once he had come, and talked so bitterly about the Korean war and the Vietnam protesters that he embarrassed everybody who wanted a good time, a few yarns, a little nostalgia, and nothing more.

And after an hour and a half at the bar, those men and their wives walked slowly and ponderously into the dining room for a terrible dinner and some of the dullest speeches most of them had heard since the last reunion.

Most of them are family men now, a few are divorced, and some have come out of the closet. They are running to fat, thinking about their golf game, their property taxes and the difficulty of raising children.

Most of them have made payments on retirement homes, and a few have even bought family plots. Their youthful liberalism, in most cases, is turning to something else as they look upon a world in which they are the movers and shakers, or their generation is, and they don't like what they see.

All the same, with every exception made, let no one call them anything less than heroes. They were plucked from everyday lives and sent out to fight a cruel and dirty but necessary war.

From hell they came back, bringing with them the greatest prize that any war can offer its soldiers, the only prize that counts in spite of words and ambitions, dreams and hopes, the one great prize: their own lives.